The History of My Body

Anomaly

An anomaly deviates from a norm,
is difficult to recognize or classify.
Anomaly is a series which publishes
heterodox, eccentric and heretical
works. Mashing fact with fiction,
poetry with philosophy, fish with
fowl, *Anomaly* is a laboratory of
unprecedented writings.

a re.press series

The History of My Body

Larissa Bird

re.press Melbourne 2012

re.press

PO Box 40, Prahran, 3181, Melbourne, Australia
http://www.re-press.org
© the author 2012
The moral rights of the authors have been asserted
First published 2012

National Library of Australia Cataloguing-in-Publication entry

Bird, Larissa.

The history of my body / Larissa Bird.

9780987268204 (pbk.)

Series: Anomaly.

Subjects: Bird, Larissa.
Women authors, Australian.
Autobiographical fiction.

A828.4

Designed and Typeset by A&R
Typeset in Sabon

Printed on-demand in Australia, the United Kingdom and the United States
This book is produced sustainably using plantation timber, and printed in the destination market on demand reducing wastage and excess transport

God deliver us from anybody who wishes to serve Him and thinks about her own dignity and fears to be disgraced.... No poison in the world so slays perfection as these things do....

St. Teresa of Avila

CONTENTS

DERIVATIVE

I always assumed I wanted to go back in.

Abandoned to life by my mother, her warm body made derelict by my rapid growth. Ripped into a permanent struggle against the oxygen that would painfully inflate my lungs until death. How I screamed until my mouth was full, my body warm, my backside rinsed of the filth in which I saturated myself. I thought I wanted to return to that place where I need not breathe, eat, shit, think for myself—my pleasure, my being, fused with mother. Reliant and defenceless, willed to take comfort in the stench of life. I wonder if getting probed deep in the abdomen fuses me again? I return to my filth—primal, bored ecstasy—when we cradle each other in a mattress soaked in sweat and mucous; this is where I live now. Together we breathe, eat, shit, forcing our bodies into one: I won't leave until I'm abandoned.

Where do I exist then, when I fuse myself? Where is my father? I remember how his liquid gave me life, how it caked yellow along the walls of my mother's uterus—the heavy thrust of his hips creaming her blood with his phlegm until some strange magic happened. I danced with my creators, rattled inside her abdomen while he finished himself off. His charm and her gentle allure made for paranormal activity—as though it was logical that expressing salty fluid into a dark cavity would make alien life.

This was where I began.

But I don't remember beginning, I don't remember those tragedies that are said to have shaped me, like when my mother turned her back on me, when I first saw myself in the mirror, when my father unleashed his desire to fuse with my body, when I realised that I would continue on until my fragile body submits itself to whatever compels it. Neither do I recall grandiose flashes, moments of catharsis, emancipation or ecstasy. I only remember existing, some ridiculous space in-between the fictions we tell ourselves about life's trajectory: milestones, traumas, divisions. Past, present, future. I have rarely seen this space abstracted. I have never heard it spoken about; but I know that the story of my life, the history of my body, is not a series of ruptures, but a system of flux that has no real limit.

* * *

I come from the suburbs of Melbourne, Australia, from a family who are nothing and everything like yours. Their aspirations for satisfaction have never been realised, their egos have been tricked into denial, sublimation and ignorance. Nothing—but everything—has been an issue. I saw no starvation, nakedness, poverty, turmoil, trauma—but I did. You probably won't believe me. I'm white, middle-class, and I won't ever come to your attention. I have a mother, a father, two sisters and a brother. That's perfection, isn't it? Three refrigerators, thirteen years of schooling, four sacraments, but only one computer.

At five months, my mother began to bleed. My conception had undoubtedly been accidental. My brother was only twenty-two months old and was, euphemistically speaking, a handful. He regularly went missing, screamed and flailed as though my mother's attempts to bathe him were an act of torture, took pleasure in breaking glass windows and, once, even managed to use all the frustrated force packed in his tiny developing muscles to flip his adult-sized bed against the door of his room. My mother and father struggled—like most—in the early days of their family. I have no doubt the undue stress of an accidental conception only intensified the emotional strain upon my parents. Because of the threatened miscarriage, my mother was forced into bed for the rest of her pregnancy. She was told to not move, even shower. She was told not to care for her precocious first-born. So she lay patient, passive in a hospital bed, for four full months, so that I could be born at all.

With my mother in hospital, my father was left alone to care for his son. The stress of it all, of watching his subjects crumble beneath him, unleashed a toxic force within his body. He could no longer digest food; it began to leave him in a burning river of black milk. His bowels wanted out. He called in help, his mother-in-law, so his son would be taken care of. He would sit on the toilet for hours, essaying to evacuate himself of his improperly absorbed food, clutching the toilet seat, his rectum burning with the acid of providence. His weight dropped so low he soon found himself in hospital with my mother—the mortifying dance of his syrupy liquid and her fertile blood tuned to a death waltz—my own body a residue of the powers of their fluids.

What a rude awakening my becoming must have been. Especially for those who had hoped for nothing more than an ordinary life, untainted.

Then I was born and came into the world, a healthy child for a growing family. The stress of my beginning was quickly forgotten. Life for them returned to something close to ordinary—except, perhaps, for me. I did not like the endless onslaught of my functioning. It would dawn upon me, quite suddenly, in the play yard of my kindergarten, in the living room of my grandparents' house, in the bath when I was left alone to wash. I would think, "How could you leave me like this?" My tears were silenced, my pain ignored, my cries never respected. It was meaningless to them. Perhaps it is the acoustics of the scream that makes us hate the sound, the way it grates on the ear. But the scream is a voice of reason. It is a violent, rational reaction to flaunt anxiety: listen to me!

I have a memory: I am in my crib and hear the sounds of my parents talking in the room next to mine. The tone of my father's voice excites me and I stand up in my cot, anxious for him to embrace me. He comes to me, raises me up in his great hands, holds me and kisses me gently, then places me back down in my cot, my body awash with his warmth.

* * *

I began my life on the fringe, between the city and the country, in a concrete puddle of monstrous powerlines, paddocks, parks coated in yellow grass and never-ending highways. This place seems only to conjure the definition of the incompetent—but it is more complicated than that. They called themselves the working-middle class; they retreated to the leafy, quasi-utopia when confronted by their shortcomings in early adulthood. But, on the surface at least, this place had a certain charisma. Long, faux-curving bicycle paths snaked into the nearby sub-temperate rainforest. The area was densely covered in old gum trees and was home to lorikeets, kookaburras and hundreds of possums. When it rained, the air would become heavy with the smell of wet eucalyptus, mounds of yellow possum shit and black soil, a rich fragrance found only in Australia.

My house was no different than any other in the neighbourhood. Forged out of an incestuous fantasy, a million brothers and sisters with the same face, windows, gardens and fences, a hemizygous deformity. Two living areas to fulfil bourgeois desires: one room formal, the other recreational (the thousands of names for such a stupid room: family room, sun room, rumpus room). Open-plan kitchen, two pokey bedrooms, one study, one master suite for the rulers of the house—open fire and en suite included. Chairs, tables and bed-frames were constructed out of particleboard or pine, stained to give the appearance of wealth. The home was kept spotlessly clean at all times. The carpet: a still pond; the curtains: crisp, the colour of champagne; the sink: a shrine to the marvels of stainless steel. Tones were neutral, an ice cream sundae of vanilla, strawberry, milk chocolate, banana. Long sticks were placed in giant stone vases, sheets and underwear had to be ironed. Refrigerators and washing machines were kept in separate rooms to stop their talk from drowning the silence.

* * *

The refrigerator and pantry were continuously stocked with traditional foodstuffs derived from the customs of our impoverished ancestors, and had to be secured with locks to stop the children from gorging themselves. White bread, white flour, potatoes, bananas, cheddar cheese, butter, milk, sausages, steaks, chops, chicken drumsticks, onions and crackers. Breakfast was brown and white, dinners and lunches were shades of yellow, orange and burnt brown. My singular source of midday nourishment for fifteen years: a heavily buttered sandwich, laden with ham and cheese, softened by the acrid taste of reconstituted juice and followed by a dark, bitter, red apple.

We lived in a time warp, a clandestine cult that had never heard of foreign cuisine or the better effects of globalisation. My father, as master of the house, refused change or variety to his diet. The staid dinner menu has remained fixed since my parents married some years ago: Mondays were burnt lamb chops and soggy vegetables left in the steamer for too long; Tuesday grilled black sausages and buttered bread; Wednesday burnt chops again; Thursday pasta; on Fridays we ate either store-bought frozen meals or take-away. The daily doses of sugar, refined grains and preservatives saw the entire family develop small potbellies that continue to grow. A constantly lethargic, bored, listless little family—until somebody opened up a bag of Doritos and the anaesthetic wore off.

Whatever passion existed before their engagement quickly dried up when my mother was duly satiated by the regulated thrustings of my father. Youthful ignorance turned into acceptance of circumstance. Imaginings could no longer exist in their material world and the sacred was repressed for the infinite. Both maintained their edification from age sixteen—their encyclopaedia composed of televisions, corporate mottos, business contracts and bank statements. Knowledge was sublimated into purchase: cars, boats, bagless vacuum cleaners, a swimming pool, a swing set for the children. Small holidays and mid-priced perfumes were gifted according to schedule—time was divided to ensure life was recognised and celebrated at the appropriate hour. Of course, one need not question the situation—it simply was, is, and always will be. The theatre of monotony on a stage of genetic mutation: *my favourite things*, glamour photography, capitalist art movements, the concerned and diligent collection of facts, statistics and data, lottery tickets, engraved jewellery. The small break that came after the first bursts of love signalling the end of passion and the beginning of a soothing, melancholic plateau.

The home, refuge for the daily grind of schooling and employment, was a scab to be compulsively picked at—a sore point that irritatingly reminded my parents of the shapeless children who lived there. Follow the rules and growth will be fostered, punish and children will learn, attend church every Sunday morning and you will be Good. Friends were rarely allowed in: they disrupted the clean order with activities that inflicted a violent break on the happy schedule. My body was their subject, my functions, appearance, behaviour controlled and maintained under their loving guardianship. Messes were to be immediately seen-to; anything left behind was promptly disposed of. My father enjoyed heaving the stinking, green garbage bin into the house and would, in one fell swoop, throw every unkempt item into his fetid, green void. I have little to show from my childhood—creations, writings, diaries and homemade trinkets now rest in landfill, beneath the care of powerlines.

Naturally, items of economic value were of greater importance. In their honour, a shrine was purchased and built according to a book of instructions. A new metal museum for the television, the bicycle, the shoe, the school textbook, the computer processor and the beloved newspaper. A sacred place to hold those things that cost time, whose coming-to-being was marked on the monthly certificates of expenditure. This catalogue for the rapid achievements of technology, the growth of my feet, the number of toothbrushes I have owned. Behold dozens of rotting machines: printers, scanners, a bag full of keyboards. Sweep away an anthology of arachnids to study the rate of inflation—truth will be revealed in those dirty piles of catalogues, see how the price of mince meat has gone up 50% in five years! Learn from the grand collection of bikes, deflated tyres and rusted chains in memory of the quick legs that once pedalled them in unison.

* * *

Where did wild passion and absurdity intervene in this homogenous world? Paradoxically, they lived in the offspring, the derivatives of suburbia: angry older brother, mischievous fraternal twin-sisters—and the confused girl in the middle. We insisted on the presence of animals in the home and turned the backyard into a zoo for cats, dogs, lovebirds, a turtle. We dragged our parents out to the cinema, to restaurants, to parties. We introduced them to the parents of our friends and expanded their social network; we brought discussions of literature, the arts, mathematics and science to the table. We interrogated the outside world, demanding to learn its functions, creations and cultures. The travels and adventures of strange figures seemed so beyond my own, repetitive life at home that I questioned their existence— thinking everyone *must* have returned home to routine meals, bathtimes, bedtimes, scheduled television, chores. I was frightened by chaos, I refused to sleep over at friends' houses, could not shit anywhere but in the sanctity of my home. Excursions outside school made me nervous, strange food shocked my body into hysteria. I broke down often.

* * *

I had difficulty learning the time: what day of the week it was or how the hands of the clock, in fact, signified the movement of planets through the solar system. Disoriented, I was told Christmas was coming—but it seemed to take forever for my presents to arrive. I must have asked one thousand times, "Is it my birthday yet?" I knew I had a birthday, but was unaware of its occasion until my mother handed me a pile of gifts and told me to blow out the candles. Of course, the surprise of living through a day of novelty made me euphoric. The passing of seasons, days, hours, years, via my growth, perplexed me. Staring at my parents' formal living room, the couches looked different to how I had previously remembered them. My home was forever misleading. This was not my furniture, my room, my kitchen; I had simply been dropped in here, without notice, by an indiscriminate stork.

My mother would read to me, but it was never enough. I had to teach myself to satisfy the gnawing demand. Much to my older brother's dismay, I pulled ahead and was called clever—but that only caused me greater torture. The announcement set him on a quest to reinstate the natural order of our birth. He would threaten to break me in half, holding my head down under his elbow and twisting my arms behind my back. I was ugly, fat, a monster—he threw me against his bed and blackened my eyes, bruised my collar bone, suffocated me in my sleep and tripped me up when I wasn't looking. He ripped at the skin of my forearm, what he called a bloody Chinese burn. Nevertheless, my passion to learn and comprehend persisted. I was obsessed with reading and forced myself to absorb the symbols on every sign, letter or book that I came upon—just to know how to pronounce and contemplate what they meant. I retreated to my room and left my brother raging outside, taken by the mysteries of the universe: extraterrestrials, the brain, gravity, conspiracy, crime. I wondered if I might be abducted one day, beamed up into a space ship and never returned. This thought caused some panic; I often hallucinated that aliens might be coming for me, but still I prayed for it happen—begging Jesus to Please Show Me The Space Craft.

I grew and grew, upwards and outwards. I sought pleasure through food, through the opening in my face. I was rewarded for my growth with an endless supply of whitestuffs, submerged in hot oil, drenched in salt. Eating felt like fusion—for a moment, at least—until my abdomen burned, my poor intestines heaved from the weight of yellow starch, my body exhausted from the empty energy. Where else to source bodily pleasure in this concrete wasteland but from fried hope, dreams, Americana? I loved Christmas even more than I loved to stuff my face. Each year, I would receive at least a dozen toys, each wrapped separately to increase the duration of my pleasure; the end of the process some predestined melancholia. I obtained most of the gifts that I demanded: a doll with secret compartments for glitter, stickers and ribbons; a Barbie that rode a bicycle; a collection of toy unicorns; a video game console; an assortment of dresses; an electronic creature, covered in hair, that spoke when you gave it the correct commandments. None of these items caused me to feel anything less than perpetually bored—save for the burst of joy at unwrapping the gift. Babies and dogs at least know the wealth of simple items, the sound of crunching paper, the roll of an empty milk bottle, the rattle of a salt shaker—far more interesting objects than a doll whose only function is to store stickers under its palm.

As I grew, I managed to stretch like a rubber band, helped by an infinite schedule of structured physical activity, happy play and youthful metabolism. I liked my body suspended in water, the feel of floating, having freedom from the earth. I liked to dance and flip, jump, hop, speed down roadways, push through wind and water—sublimate and transgress my body, train it, force its limits. But I was trapped in it. I couldn't master total control over my muscles, limbs, fingers or toes. I couldn't eat when I wanted, sleep when it felt necessary, play when I sought it, piss when my bladder was full. I had to wait for permission, wait for adults to authorise the use of my body as necessary. My growth was retarded into submission to my environment: cheap mass-produced clothes, monotonous animated video tapes, endless piles of dolls and toys to mimic the activities of the hermetic home atmosphere. After I had achieved the necessary milestones—walking, talking, swimming, riding a bike—there seemed to be little left for me to do but wait. What joy was there left to achieve, in the eyes of my parents, when all that awaited them was the detachment of puberty, the anti-climax of secondary education and the slow, tortuous growth into adulthood.

At the mercy of my brain, I was forever assailed by its technique of intimidation. I began to develop nervous reactions, neuroses and affectations. My mouth would twist and dart to-and-fro across my face whenever I conjured some nasty truth. My fingers stiffened into violent coils, each knuckle bent over the other when I felt exposed. My eyes seemed to be separated from my body and would blink continuously, as though I couldn't bear to keep my face relaxed for more than a second. My feet would clamp, my breath became quick and shallow. I thought other people could hear what I was thinking, that my parents somehow knew all my secrets. I would sometimes respond to myself—occasionally out loud—asking to please be left alone. The power of my mind, the fact that I couldn't control it, horrified me more than anything else. I thought Satan might know some of my secret thoughts too, I was particularly afraid of him. In my piety, I believed he had the ability to take souls from young children, so I would tempt Him with the thought "you can have my soul, Satan", but then quickly reply to myself, "Oh, God, take it back!" I played this mind-game once when I was eating dinner and a large wad of food became stuck in my throat. My brother had to pound on my back until it dislodged from my windpipe. This brief moment of suffocation caused me to feel even more fearful of the Devil and, following this incident, if the thought of him popped up, I would have to stop my entire body from moving—put down the fork, lower the pencil, jump off the slide—and stand very still, with my hands behind my back, breathing softly, staring straight ahead. I would pray for him to leave me alone, promise that I wouldn't tempt him with the offer of my soul anymore. He never left me alone. His presence continued until I became an atheist.

* * *

My first nightmare occurred when I was three years old.

I was lying in my bed, my eyes cast upward to the ceiling. A fat, brown spider sat, perched high in the corner, his two front legs twitching, mocking me—knowing I am trapped in my unconscious state. He works carefully, spinning a web that edges closer and closer to my face. His frenzied, thin pricks construct each hinge and hook to support his web, this new tomb for my mouth. I arch my jaw open, hoping a scream will come out—but it is too dry, my throat is clamped from fear and from thirst. He spins thin white streaks across my face, I can't escape; it moves back and forth all over me, I am frozen.

The nightmare mutates as I mature; the spider became an aeroplane. In this dream, I am always in a field, my body exposed to the open, blue sky. I can't go anywhere; the sky will know where I am. I waft through this vision, until I gaze up and see a 747 slice through the infinite blue sheet, hurtling toward me like a fireball. The plane is graceful, slow—but determined to get me. I try to run, but my body is stunned from the exposure—where could I go, where could I run to and be safe? The plane grows louder, the engine fills me until I can't breathe anymore—the white cylinder barrels toward me until it comes. But I cannot move, I struggle to breathe, my tongue grates like sandpaper across the roof of my mouth. Again, I am frozen.

* * *

I must indulge myself for a moment and address you directly, reader. This after all is the history of my life, my body—a brief moment of indiscretion won't cause too much harm. What is it to *recall* memories, how can someone write a history of their self without prompting questions of accuracy? Memories: the word lends itself to suspicion, devoid of authenticity, evidence—pure subjectivity. I do not claim to have recalled anything—any event that I have remembered in my lifetime has always been with me, inside my head. But it has been that as I have grown, the shape and definition of the memory, my understanding of it, has changed. Things may be forgotten, moments, conversations, facts, answers—but the sum of my existence is bound by my memory. It has constructed who I am and how I recall it. Through my body and mind is my history.

In the beginning, my most frightening experiences were the regular dreams I had of my mother and father fucking me.

We were in the TV room. She was dressed in a comforting terry towelling gown that was stained with cigarette burns and thinned from years of wear. I dreamt of her smell, a familiar musty, sour smell. It moved across the tips of my nostrils, an acrid aroma with the hint of digested garlic—somehow soothing in its gentle, familiar subtlety—the result of an evening spent in front of the television, gorging on corn chips and cheap box wine. She dances drunkenly, clutching the pole of a lamp—her hips thrusting up against the thin pole. Her groin presses against the black bar. I know what she is doing and what she is trying to feel—I have done the same thing myself. She clutches my arm, still gripping the pole with her free hand. Feverishly, she rips off my clothes until I stand naked before her heaving, drunken, wretched body. She arches her neck back violently and her jaw disconnects, like rubber, the flesh dropping onto her breast. She becomes a mechanical clown, slowly rotating her head from side to side, taunting me to put my head inside her gaping mouth. Quickly, she reaches out and shoves my head inside her face, clamping down with her rotten, yellow teeth.

Twisted pleasure, because I like the feel of her soft body up against mine. My head is in her mouth, but she embraces me into her dressing gown. I want to merge with her gown and lie in it forever.

* * *

It seems inevitable that becoming father means becoming obsessed with matters of defecation. Mine readily announced, to the entire family, each time he needed to retreat into the WC. He was the commentator on his progress, as though a great ceremony were taking place before him: the passing of his waste, an event of global significance. This impressed my sisters and I who, as small children, found it hilarious. We revelled in the process, barracking him on whenever he took a shit. His excrement had a strange smell, an odd stuffiness that was not unlike mildew—a room that had not been aired with the added presence of sweaty, wheezing, gym clothes. When he was finished he would wash his hands for an eternity, then leave the bathroom door wide open so that the musty smell could waft throughout the entire house. My brother followed suit and copied this territorial method, though his shit had a terrible smell that made the entire house reek. For a while he took powder protein supplements, in some vain effort to boost his adolescent muscles, although the only effect it had was that it made his shit reek like rotting corpses.

How does a daughter cope when she feels uncomfortable around her father? Every girl loves her father; even if he is the worst tyrant, she will still suffer from the curse of devotion. Until around the time I started menstruating, I oscillated between feelings of love and admiration with some disquiet; after that, I simply began to hate him outright. I remember thinking that my father was the greatest man in the world, that so few others could match his shrewd outlook, his sociability, his diligence with money, and even his control over life matters. I was easily flattered by his compliments, enjoyed the power of his company, and regularly turned to him for advice, as all children will naturally do around a father who provides something for his children. He spent time with us, taught me how to ride a bicycle, how to drive a car and how to light a fire, how to manage a bank account and file a tax return. He enjoyed sharing his wisdoms through repetition, telling me over and over how, as a small boy, he had stolen a tennis racket from a shop—only to be dragged back by his mother to apologise. Now, because of this, he was a better man. He often liked to ask if I wanted to marry him; a request that made me giggle, but still utter a definite "No!"

"Don't you want to marry me? You have such pretty ears, they look like a shell".

Even as a five year old, I knew that daughters are not supposed to marry their fathers.

* * *

The sound, smell and feel of my genitals both fascinated and shamed me. At school camp I lay awake in my bed, gently fondling and playing with the lips of my cunt. I shifted my fingers through, crippled with the fear that somebody might hear the soft sound. I moved as quietly as I could, breathing in short bursts through my nose, listening to the rhythm of the bush that played outside the tent. The smell of my unwashed body, salty and caked from a day in the dirt, rose up from out of the sleeping bag where I imagined it to hover like a dirty, knowing cloud around my body. I felt as though the whole world must have known what I was doing, but was duly unable to stop. In the morning I made my bed carefully, in case an adult straightened it and discovered the familiar smell of low tide. Instead, to my horror and shame, the teacher unzipped the sleeping bag and opened it up completely, "to air it out!" she said. Her action promptly ripped my body open; every secret I kept chained inside was plastered on the walls for all to see. I vomited all over the ground and a nervous breakdown ensued. I was rewarded with a teddy bear, my teachers assuming that I simply felt homesick.

My friend Sabine and I used to lie in the middle of the school oval with her brother Nicolas—he was perhaps two years older—and he would lower our underwear and look at our vaginas, rubbing them and thrusting his hips up against our bodies. I felt I was doing something sinful, my parents would not approve—this was my fear—but I would retreat to my bedroom and masturbate over what Nicolas and his sister had done on the grass, our activities hidden because we lay at the bottom of the hill. I liked to pretend that I might go over to see Sabine and Nicolas one day to play; only he would take me into his bathroom and take off all my clothes. Then, I would fantasise about an older woman leading me out of school and onto a train. She didn't have a face; I couldn't bring myself to picture one, I suppose I wanted her to be anonymous. She would unbutton her shirt for me and, in full view of everyone on the train, force her breasts into my mouth. I wanted to drink her milk, to taste the feel of a nipple against my tongue. I would suck my thumb when I thought about this woman, grinding my immature hips against a pillow that I placed between my legs. I would think about her cleaning me up after I defecated, hoisting my two legs over her shoulders and wiping my backside with a wet cloth while I lay and let her care for me. Never able to reach climax, I had to stop after short bursts of these fantasies. I was afraid of the iniquity of my thoughts, that someone might discover the truth and punish me. I knew that Jesus and Mary could hear all my secrets and so, every time I masturbated, I would rise up on my knees in bed, hunched over like a human tent with the blanket draped across my bent back, and apologise profusely to them both, silently begging forgiveness when I committed an act upon my body.

I prayed often.

* * *

My sisters and I suffered from terrible eczema throughout our childhood. We were treated to a nightly dose of cortisone and zinc creams that were slathered over our bodies in an attempt to lock in moisture. It never quite worked; the stress of our living conditions and our impoverished diet meant we saw little improvement in the thick scales that covered our arms and legs. My youngest sister Lydia, in particular, suffered brutally from the wounds over her body—she could not desist from picking at the scabs that her skin produced, and was not allowed to swim because of it—sometimes having to be bathed with a damp sponge because the water was simply too painful. My mother would have to wrap her in cotton bandages to try and keep the wounds coated in cream, safe from the promise of her wandering fingernails.

We would call Lydia 'mummy' because of this, a name she detested, but nonetheless found funny because of its connotations. She would cackle, "I'm the mummy and you're the baby". Her twin, Carly would often play at Lydia being her mummy, wrapping her body around Lydia and screaming at the top of her voice, "Mummy!" This game made me feel odd, to see Carly's legs wrapped around my other sister, her groin pressed tightly up against her thigh.

We shared a tiny room: two bunk beds pushed up against adjacent pale pink walls, the floor always covered in toys, books and animal hair, the cupboards bleeding out rivers of clothing until my father dumped the lot into the street and made us clean it up. We would usually cram into one bed at night, snuggling tightly into each other, tucking our dolls and bears into the opposite end of the bed. My sisters would show each other their genitals and ask me to touch them, a game we usually played in the secrecy of the night. Even though they were younger than me, I was almost always outmatched by the strength of their robust personalities, relating to them with the same rollercoaster of hatred and love possessed by most sisters.

Our school was located on the outskirts of the bush. A small country school had been selected for our education on the basis of its small class sizes, quiet location and close-knit community. Each day we submitted to an arduous car ride away from the dangers of the suburbs into the sanctity of the bush and my small, red brick primary school. My parents loved the Australian landscape, but could not manage to abandon themselves to living nestled beneath the trees—the fear of bushfires too prevalent in their mind after their house had nearly burnt down some ten years earlier. So we studied in the quiet forest and returned to the suburbs each day. I liked being submerged in the musty smell of brown horses, dry paddocks and old eucalyptus—the melody of kookaburras, whipbirds and magpies regularly lulled me into a sleepy haze with the boredom of afternoon studies.

As it was a Catholic school, we were prescribed a heavy dose of religious instruction alongside the usual curriculum. Nuns often visited to teach us about the power of the mind—how God would speak to us and guide us throughout our lives. He will tell us what we want to be, what we should become when we grow up. The great question asked of every ten year old—*what do you want to be?*—would be nurtured in the care of the Lord, and an answer would be made known to us with the passing of time. One Nun regularly visited our class. She was a feisty older woman who dressed in pastel tones, woollen jumpers with knitted kangaroos, and wore her white hair impossibly short.

She explained to us how God had told her she should be a Sister:

She had been with a man, he was handsome in his youth, he had taken her on a date to the cinema and asked her to marry him—but she heard God's voice in the dark auditorium. He said she should not be here; she should be in

God's house. She told us that celibacy meant your heart was with God, that your physical body was only a vessel for His work, not for sexual pleasure. She told us how she worked for charities, for sick children, for the elderly. Her life was fulfilling, she was able to travel all over the world and spread the word of God. She told us that she bumped into the man who proposed to her many years later and said that he had become ugly, she was glad in her decision to become a sister of God. I thought how wonderful to be relieved of passion and dirty desire; charity certainly seemed a noble path to follow, one that would make me feel good in the eyes of Jesus, the one who could hear all my thoughts. I saw the attention given to Princess Diana upon her death and felt for the neglect of Mother Teresa—the only photo of her that was published was the one that included the Princess. I felt betrayed by the life of the layman, I felt God was speaking to me, that he was telling me to be good and charitable, and follow the path of this woman. I thought, "Perhaps I, too, will become a Nun".

* * *

Sex percolated through me like radioactive waste. A neurotoxin—nothing disgusted me more. Some of my schoolteachers seemed to know of its effect; one in particular liked to drape herself in clothing designed to cover as little soft tissue as possible. She would bend over her desk, calling the eyes of her students to the gap between her breasts, a dark hole for us to dive into. I blushed every time I saw that hole, I was embarrassed by my body. Hers was a spectacular foreign wilderness, an object she flaunted with pride, and I could not wrench my eyes away from it. She would paralyse me and I became her victim. An animal caught in the trap of a bright light by a vicious body. The simple experience of her body in my mind, she knew about it, our intersubjective fantasy for the space between her flesh. She liked to seduce my father on parent-teacher nights, winking and tossing her hair, while telling him what a good pupil I was. He spent most of the session staring at her breasts through her bent down body, hanging fruit for hungry eyes.

At age eight, I made a secret pact with myself to stop making eye contact with her. She overwhelmed me with her strange stares, her lingering eye, her engulfing chest. She would come up behind us in class and run her fingers through our hair, commenting on how silky it was. "What shampoo do you use? You smell wonderful!" I wanted her to do this to me, but it pushed a black wave through my body—I became a dirty girl when she did it, ashamed and embarrassed by the very presence of my being. When she escorted us, with a group of mothers, to the local pool for swimming class, she insisted on helping me undress. I often forgot my swimming bag and, despite my refusal, she would force me to borrow a spare swimsuit from the school office. I lightly soiled my underwear to thwart her, but she continued to dress me for the lesson all the same and, upon finding the putrid streaks, hung my underwear inside out on the peg so that the shit was on display for the entire changeroom to see.

* * *

In the quiet sanctity of the bush, my tiny school revelled in its wonderfully proactive safety house programme. Despite the distance of home from school, my family signed up— my mother needed something to relieve her of afternoon boredom—and we happily attached a yellow house to our letterbox to let children in trouble know that there were no

Paedophiles inside. We had regular classroom discussions about the purpose of the little yellow sign, how many children make use of it regularly. We were told that perhaps a friend trips and hurts himself, maybe the chain falls off your bike, you might not have enough money for a bus fare, maybe someone tries to snatch you into their white van. Anything can happen.

I was already too well aware of the kinds of emergencies that were of high risk to children left alone. My father took an interest in showing me newspaper clippings of various young girls who had been kidnapped, raped, mutilated and murdered. He told me what happened to them, regularly calling me over to the kitchen table after we had all eaten dinner. He sat in his chair while I stood by his side, and he recounted what bad men liked to do to young girls. When my sisters started school, he began to lecture the three of us. He told me about Mr Cruel, the danger of strange men, how one little girl had met her fate—she was found dead, mutilated and abused, thrown in a dam and drowned because he had weighted her backpack with bricks. Holding a crumpled newspaper in his hand, he pointed out her picture, showing how she looked just like me: dark blonde hair, smiling brown eyes, light skin, a shy smile. I was severely warned never to wander alone for fear my body would be violated, ripped open—removed from the control and care of my father. He hugged me tightly once he had finished telling me about these girls. I was blank, empty, afraid some man might try to climb in through the window and snatch me.

I was in Grade Three, my best friend was Sabine. We were inseparable. She came from a large Belgian Catholic family that had immigrated to Australia in the mid-1980s. She was short with dirty blonde hair, and always smelled of the onion soup she ate for lunch. Her mother was a slight, graceful woman with an androgynous appearance that made her seem enchanted. She reminds me now of Patti Smith, with long, frizzy, grey hair, a warmly wrinkled face and slim frame that she carried with poise. Her presence relaxed me and caused me to talk with a certain air of maturity. I heard myself beginning sentences with phrases like, "Well, that is rather interesting ..." or "Oh yes, please, Madame". Even then, I wanted to feel more refined than the odd classlessness of my very Australian family.

Sabine's father reminded me of my own. His friendly face acted as a mask for the arrogance and fury simmering under the surface. Sabine would regularly come to school with strange bruises across her back, a cut hand, a black eye. We never spoke about our fathers, but we knew we came from the same stock and needed one another from the instant we met. Quickly, the force of our bond disturbed our teachers and we were promptly split apart. When we managed to be together again, we forgot the world around us, rarely listening to the lesson at hand. Consumed only by the depth of our conversation—usually on the subject of the universe, horses and dragons—we lazed across each other on the carpet, running our fingers through each other's hair.

I don't recall how it started, there was probably no singular moment that brought Sabine and I together. What I remember is the time we spent perched in the corner of a toilet cubicle, dresses pushed over our heads, knickers around our ankles. Sabine liked to touch me, giggling as she pushed her hand gently into the folds of my skin. I liked to do the same to Sabine, lifting the edge of her T-shirt over her head and kissing the skin of her chest. She smelled like onions and urine, a combination of the soup and her poor hygiene. We would stare into each other's pupils and press our lips together—the game being never to lose eye contact.

These were formative romantic moments, locked inside the windy bathroom over lunch, embroiled in the indeterminacy of our action. Our frivolities would last for up to an hour; we would leave once the bell sounded, our hands coated with traces of urine and excrement from placing our fingers in spaces they were not meant to be. I would often dry-retch after seeing what was over my hands, surprised that sexual contact meant interacting with waste. Yet we continued to retreat to the toilets when it suited us, our secret ours for months. Until disaster struck.

When a girl named Lucy, the daughter of an upstanding, thirteen-member-strong, Catholic family, uncovered our mischief one day in the toilet, everything changed.

Lucy shared with her parents the tale of her encounter, who shared it with the parents' association, who shared it with my family. It filtered through to the school principal, local priest, nuns and, of course, our fellow classmates. The tiny, close community I belonged to ruptured into a crazed panic. Meetings were held, announcements were made through private letters to every family. I mutated into Pandora—nobody would come near me for fear of contamination. I accidentally knocked into a mother in the corridor and she recoiled in horror, the stroke of my passing causing her to hiss involuntarily: "Get away from me!"

My mummy says I can't play with you because you're dirty.

Parents forbade their children to play with either Sabine or I, so we were left alone, ripped apart from our small world by our act of intimate curiosity. Naturally, I was also forbidden to play with Sabine, and we were carefully watched by both teachers and classmates. Everyone meticulously maintained their post, ensuring that we were nowhere near each other. Although I loved her, I still felt that what I had done was shameful, wrong. I am a bad child—a sinner at ten years old. So I spent my break in complete solitude, ashamed and belittled. I had been excited to turn ten that year, double digits was something to celebrate—but instead I spent my birthday wondering what would happen if I let my body fall from the church tower, from the window of my bedroom, what if I jumped out of my parents' speeding car. I thought: "Too bad about the child-lock, I would have to wind down the window and reach my arm out".

Sabine ran up to me where I was sitting alone on the bench and whispered into my ear. She led me over to a brick wall and showed that if I banged my head hard enough against the surface, it would crack open and bleed. We did it together. She drove her head so forcefully into the wall that it split open and red liquid gushed down her face. This just made her laugh. A teacher discovered us and tore the two of us apart—the shock of blood over our faces, the laughter in our eyes made people stand back with their mouths agape— "Devils!"

* * *

The adults, especially my father and the school principal, were very intrigued by what *exactly* had transpired between Sabine and me, demanding to know every detail. We were harassed on a weekly basis by those seeking a catalogue of the individual moments that had slipped between us, until we were exhausted of all the evidence. Sometimes my father threatened to take me to the police station to file a report. Sabine had committed a crime upon my body, he said. I had shamefully lied to him, claiming Sabine had forced herself upon me without my consent. I felt that I had betrayed Sabine, the girl I loved, by admitting this—but it was the only way

I could preserve myself. The best way out of my dilemma was to ensure that I was removed of any guilt, of any sin. I was unaware how loaded it was to make such a claim, how disturbing it would seem to the adults around me. Though I doubt that admission of fault would have made my situation any better—but I realised many years later that the lie of molestation added an extra tinge of perversity.

* * *

Several months later, the school principal called me into his office for yet another interrogation. I had withdrawn from my studies, cried excessively in class and was still shunned by my peers at lunch and playtimes. I had begun to prefer sitting in solitude on the bench anyway. At that point, everybody seemed just stupid. He wanted to know why this was happening, why I cried so often. He made my mother and teacher attend this meeting as well. Once again, I had to repeat what had transpired between Sabine and me.

I stared through his dusty horizontal blinds and said, rather vaguely, that we "played with each other".

"Where? Where did she touch you? Use the right words, please."

I had learned about the word *vulva* during a sex education class earlier in the year. The woman running the class said it sounded like Volvo and that thinking of this was a good way to remember the name. That sounded funny to me at the time, but now the word made me want to melt into the floor and disappear. I forced it out of my mouth:

"We touched each other on the Volvo."

"You mean vulva."

My teacher stared at me furiously, demanding to know if Sabine and I had done anything since we had been caught.

By chance we had ended up in the stationery cupboard together, searching for paintbrushes the previous Friday, during afternoon craft. We hadn't done anything, but she didn't believe me.

"Yes, you did. Just admit it. What did you do in that cupboard?"

I repeated over and over that nothing had happened. My mother began to cry and asked the principal if perhaps the sex education classes had anything to do with my behaviour. He had no answer for that, but I knew it wasn't true. I wanted to say that Sabine and I had been playing with each other for months before those classes, but thought better of it. They wanted more information, what else had we done, where had she put her mouth, her fingers, how long for? I repeated that Sabine knew Judo and had forced me to participate. The interrogation continued until I broke down, hysterical, retching over the floor of his office, my mother unable to console me or calm me down. She had to half-carry me back to her car and take me home early from school.

That night, my father again tried to drag me to the police station, convinced that Sabine had committed some heinous crime. "She is a paedophile", he told me. I was clothed only in a nightgown, wearing no underwear under my thin cloth dress. My mother would scold me if I wore underwear to bed: "You have to let it breathe, Larissa". He gripped my arm and dragged me out to the car, throwing me in the front seat. He began to reverse violently down the drive, but in a fit of panic I managed to jump out of the moving vehicle to sprint back inside, diving as quickly as I could onto my mattress and gripping the bed post until my knuckles turned blue. I held on as tightly as I could, my legs pressed firmly together because I did not want to reveal my naked backside to anyone who came in, but I did not want to let go of the post to adjust the dress either. I screamed until my throat burned, "Just leave me alone!"

I was no longer allowed to go to the toilet by myself. Teachers thought I might try to masturbate in there, so I was accompanied every time. I was also no longer allowed to swim in the same group as Sabine, no longer allowed to share a tent with her on camping trips. My actions were under the constant supervision of both teachers and my peers. Even if Sabine and I stopped to have some brief conversation in the schoolyard, we would be accosted by a swarm of students breaking us apart with their arms—lest we started touching each other again. The teachers held a class meeting. They explained what had happened, that we were embarrassed by it and should be left alone and not be bullied because of it. With Sabine and I sitting on opposite sides of the classroom, hanging our heads in shame, the teachers told my peers that we were not allowed to play with each other and should be reminded of this if it were to happen. "Yes, you should call a teacher if you see them together."

Yet the shame of these new rules was nothing compared to the grief I felt over my love for Sabine, nor for the pleasures my body had given me. I prayed to Jesus that he might send me some relief from the burden of my sin. Instead, I was treated to the onslaught of my mind, my thoughts whirring, repetitive, over and over—I was dirty, shameful, despicable, wicked. This must be God talking and every adult could hear. I wanted to rip my clitoris out. I detested it for all the humiliation it had brought upon me. It never stopped reminding me of its presence. Each time my vulva pulsated, I would pound my hand against my groin over and over until I became so red and swollen it was painful to walk or sit.

* * *

My grandmother had given me a pair of porcelain cats from Japan. They were elegant statues, a fine pair of cream Siamese statues that stood proudly on my highest shelf—the home for my finest possessions. Alongside was a fine bone tea set, arranged in a pink chest with the names of the three sisters hand-painted on the lid in swirled writing: "*Larissa, Lydia, Carly*". There was also a handmade ragdoll from an American Indian reservation gifted to me by an aunt, and a silver jewellery box lined with pale pink satin. Inside was a tiny ballerina who danced to chimes whenever the box was opened. In it, my mother had placed a silver signet ring engraved with my initials and a tiny pair of earrings purchased in anticipation of my sixteenth birthday—the year she had decided appropriate for me to have my ears pierced. She encouraged me to display my finest possessions up high, leaving the cheaper cartoon knick-knacks on the lower shelves. She would keep some better items aside—a silver rattle from my infancy, a porcelain doll from Franklin Mint, an embroidered banner made by my grandmother, for the rare occasions when friends were invited over— and produce them an hour or so before their arrival so that I could display some of the more delicate figurines for "looking not touching".

Still gripped onto my bed, after my father had tried to drag me to the police station, I looked up at that shelf. I hastened my heavy breathing to hear if anyone was coming for me—there wasn't. My father had, in fact, left for Sabine's house. I learnt later that he stormed inside and threatened Sabine's mother to keep her filthy child away from me—although, by this time, nearly six months had passed since Sabine and I had been caught, so he had little to worry about. I unravelled my fingers from the edge of my bedframe and sat up on my mattress. I could not stop panting, hot saliva had dripped from my mouth onto the starched pillowcase below, a clear pool had formed in the crease. I stared at every precious item I had been given. Quickly, in a fit of rage, I jumped up and dragged my arm across that top shelf. With one violent swoop I forced every delicate statue onto the floor below. The sound of crashing porcelain was matched only by the bellowing of my mother. It was hard to tell what made her angrier, that I had let a girl finger me in the school toilets, or that I had broken every delicate item that marked the primal milestones I had achieved so far. The force of my aggression and act of smashing so many treasured possessions caused my parents to put me in therapy.

I had turned eleven by then, but still somehow knew that therapy meant you had lost control over your mental faculties. I was resistant to the idea: why should I be forced to tell my story over again? Naturally, the school principal referred my family to a Catholic therapist. Fortunately, my mother could afford only one session.

I attended with her one weekday afternoon and was removed from school early for the occasion—an action that always requires explanation to one's peers (I could not bring myself to tell them the truth and concocted some silly lie). I remember very little of the actual session, because I was only inside her office for a short period of time. My mother took up most of the time howling uncontrollably, while I waited outside. We left, with the counsellor insisting that we make another appointment, but my mother refused because of the expense. In the car on the way home, she told me two things the therapist had said to her:

1. It was likely that in the future I would have trouble relating to boys, and:

2. There was a chance I could grow up to be a paedophile.

For the next ten years I would not be able to even look at a child without thinking I might harm them.

ISOMORPHISMS

A morass of pavlova, barbeques, funerals, weddings, Christmas, one hundred strokes of the lip across the cheek. Not adolescent 'like they don't understand me', but chasmic nonalignment.

I must perform.

"What do you want to be when you grow up?"

I think: "Fuck off."

I answer: "A school teacher."

Perimeters of being. A recital of conversation and digestion that tastes too strong. Charred sausage soaked in tomato sauce, salty and moist, red goo running down your throat, hard meat against the cheek. Why does it feel good to swallow blackened sausage, all salt and jelly-cum-rubber? Once I dropped my sausage on the floor but I picked it up and ate it anyway because my mother only gave me enough silver for one.

I don't want dessert. My father scoops a wad of white meringue into a plastic bowl and hands me a plastic spoon. Glazed fruit falls over the edge and drips down my leg. My toes are swollen from mosquito bites. I will make myself ignored and stay quiet with this plastic pavlova and my mutant legs.

Bite into the sickly meringue, white crust morphs into

rubber and it will float over your teeth. Don't spit it out, swallow. Grinding against your enamel, saliva turns to syrup, soft foam from hard meringue. Eat it. Chewy and gooey, shiny red fruit, finish your sugar.

What is this dessert? How is it like a graceful ballerina? Whispers that she's shy and has trouble settling. Nobody will mention *those* incidents. How I'm going to have problems with boys, how I'm going to grow up to be a paedophile. No, I will be a school teacher, a nurse, a librarian. Yes, says mother, she is good with children ... my father agrees.

I choke on the syrup, tabloid news reports, an Asian invasion.

"I didn't mind Pauline."

Aboriginal footballers are good at football, there is a homosexual in the office but he works well. Finish your pavlova and we'll leave, then your spider will take you home.

Half drunk, half awake.

I want to jam my finger in my mouth and tear through the muck, swill water to wash away the thick glue stuck inside my throat. Why can't I breathe properly? The blankets are getting ripped on and ripped off, my body is exposed then hidden. Back and forth. I am lying down, legs open, mouth wide and I can't move, my lungs are squashed. I need water.

I never thought I was very attractive, but I was. Years of gymnastics sculpted my body. Long, muscular legs, a smooth torso, fresh buds. When I see photos of myself now, I see why people turned their heads toward this ten year old. My legs are tanned, lean, with the agility and arc of a woman's. My eyes are bright, naughty, desiring. I can see the pixie in them, little miss mischievous. I am becoming awake.

But my shoulders bend to face each other. They can't reach to cover the breasts that keep poking up and out. I rarely shower, I hate to shower ... the spider might be watching. A spider lurks in the corner, eight eyes wanting to know what you are doing. I wash my body quickly. Clotted uterine blood runs down my legs. It gets stuck in the drain and limps over it, stringy blood not ready to disappear. Photos of me change, my eyes are dim now. Why can't she settle? Why won't she look at me in the eye? Let me touch you, here have some pavlova.

I stare straight ahead. I have been woken up early. I hate the pajamas mum buys me. Singlets with strappy tops that fall down in the night, I wake up and I see my breasts, the spider sees my breasts. I hold tightly on to the blanket, I don't want him to pull it back and see when I am asleep. I fall unconscious still gripping the blanket, fingers clenched, toes curled. I am afraid to open my eyes. I can't sleep with the blanket pulled up against me. I can't clutch it all night in this sweltering heat. I fall asleep and I have to forget. He comes in. "What are you doing sleeping with all these blankets on?" He rips the doona out of my fingers and exposes my body. The summer dress won't cover me up. I lie there powerless. He just stands and stares, runs a hand over my head and edges it down my neck. He won't stop looking at me. He leaves the room. He doesn't turn out the light, he refuses to shut the door. If I close it, he opens it again. Lit up, open, available.

I have trouble remembering who the spider is. I think he might be out the window, up in the sky, behind the corner. My eyes deceive me, I think he is a pot plant, I think he is the dressing gown in my cupboard, he was the man who called me over the fence to come play, he was the man in the haunted house at the amusement park who wouldn't move when I walked into him. He held me close, he moved his hips, he wouldn't let go of my neck. I don't like answering the phone in case the spider calls. I don't like walking down the dark hall in case he is at the end, lurking in the corner. I am ten years old, ten years old is double digits, no more barbies, crop tops, braces, a summer of hula hoops, bicycles, Sabine and fish fingers. I hate the smell of fish fingers, it reminds me of my vomit, a vomit that tastes like fishy water.

Why does my breath smell like fish?

I get caught touching Sabine's feet. We were stroking each other with a feather in class. She liked it when I move the feather up her thigh, her breath quickened, her muscles flexed and she giggled. We are together in our own whirlpool, nobody can get in here. But I don't know that I share it, that people see everything when I walk down the street. Long lean legs thumping the footpath. I uncross my legs and he is staring. I suffocate a scream.

Nobody talks about my problem. I am the one who used the feather, who fondles herself, who might be a paedophile when I grow up because I used the feather. He keeps porn in the garage, he stares at his 8-9-10-11 year old daughter, he touches her when he thinks mother isn't looking. He touches her when mother is looking. He gave her her first kiss.

"Truth."

"Have you ever kissed someone, Larissa?"

"No."

That is a lie.

Mum starts drinking. Wine from a box is only $8. Summer is agony. It's too hot, too many barbeques, too many aunts and uncles coming over. "How are you? What are you going to be when you grow up?"

I turn thirteen. High school starts. Small shocks cause waves of tension that never dissipate. A tsunami I create to blast through myself. Possessed by the sight of a spider dangling from a thread on the ceiling—I can play pretend, but really all I can think about is that spider. Is he inside the toilet roll, waiting for my hand to grasp the paper, ready to pounce? Is he underneath my pillow, waiting until my head rests and I fall asleep? He will crawl out and enter my mouth. Is he inside the toilet, waiting for my naked backside to cover the seat, so he can strike and attack my insides? Or is he just outside the window, watching me undress?

Perfectly still, the spider knows where you are but is clever enough to keep his presence a secret. Maybe your hairs will prick up, your breath will get shallow—it will be difficult to relax—you know something isn't right, something is preventing you from letting go, from releasing the tension. To feel good, you start to poke at your body, try to let out some of the steam that is becoming increasingly compacted inside your chest. As your stomach rises and falls, your hands wander across your skin, picking at hardened scabs, peeling flesh, stray hairs, hardened calluses on your heels. You dive into your body to forget the tension, the hairs and dead skin make you forget the spider and remember yourself—but it doesn't last long. Hours might pass, hours of picking, peeling and pulling and you lift your head, your neck stiff from remaining in the same tense position, your eyes blurry from focusing on the smallest pieces of your body and you see that the spider has not left.

He keeps coming back. He wakes us up every morning. My mother keeps buying me summer pajamas, tiny shorts and loose singlets. They slide around when I sleep; a breast pokes out of the limp shirt, my lips exposed through the slack shorts. I won't let go of the blanket. My mind races— why can't I keep my body as my own, mine to have and to live in without his interference. But he is my father and he loves me. I try to forget everything, to not think a single thought for more than one second. God, I wish my mind would just shut up. He wakes me every morning—he rips back the blanket. His hands are stronger than mine. His arms are warranted in their action—I need to get up for school. It doesn't matter how tightly I hold onto my blanket. I am not, never will be, strong enough. He rips it back and sees our bodies, opened up from the flabby pajamas and a restless sleep. He steps back, inhaling our presence, rumbling in the shallow dark of the morning,

"Get up!"

He watches me shove my breast back inside its sleeve, tug awkwardly on the seam of my shorts. He won't look away. I try to swing my legs over the bed without opening them, like my ankles are tied. My pajamas are too floppy, don't bother.

I can't think about how he does this, how he stares at me, I refuse—my mind must be lying, an untruth. Fathers love their daughters.

It was my dad to whom we turned to ask permission to see a friend, for money, for help or advice. My mum is not the same. Her children speak to her the same way that he does. Like a dog, a dumb dog that knows nothing but box wine and women's television. She is only allowed a small allowance per week and has to prove how much she has spent. Every item needs a receipt, but she often forgets. She sulks in her bed, drunk, farting, a pig in a blanket—my father screams at her from rooms away, "Where is the receipt!" Somehow, it becomes my fault. He switches, ignoring her and blaming me. I was useless, he did everything—didn't we know?

Of course, he discovered that it was, in fact, his misdeed, his purchase that marked the frail line on the bank statement: 150mm type serving his declaration of war, his declaration of peace. I stole $1 from his purse and he knew. He counted everything—remembering exactly how much money he had at every moment. I was slapped violently across the backs of my knees for that, the trace of his fingers in red along the top of my calf, branded a thief. He never let my indiscretion fade, regularly reminding me of my crime. His family are his toothpicks, snapped between the dirty, yellow knobs inside his orifice. He yearns to open the gates of hell, craves our infinite subordination. Threats to set the house on fire unless it was clean, screams that the dog will be shot and disembowelled until we take better care of it. He loves to dump all our possessions out in the street and watch us scramble for them. That is his favourite trick.

But he is friendly, charming, witty in public. I am humbled by the myth of the doppelgänger, such is the force with which it takes hold of my dad. He smiles, remembers every person's name, takes notice of what is going on around him. At work, his friends ask me: "Why aren't you nicer to your dad? He loves you"; "Your dad is wonderful, your mum is just so lucky".

A social butterfly that crawls back into its cave and metamorphoses into a dirty snake. But even I am seduced by the colour of his charms, his happy laugh that warmly ripples across the room. His olive eyes twinkle and he stares at you, throwing a hand across the front of your chest and patting it reassuringly—daddy is here, darling. When photographs are taken, he always places his hand across my breastbone, making sure I am closest to him. Daddy protects me, he loves me, he wants to marry me. Safe in the arms of my father, he apes how wonderful a family can be. How did he learn to look after me like this? Where did he come from? What was he before I existed? Not a father, a husband, a son, a brother, a child, a working boy, a catcher on his cricket team, a ladies' man.

I had seen him kiss my mother, seen them fucking on the couch when they thought I was playing in my room—but even that didn't bother me. I looked on, somewhat perplexed, but amused by them actually playing at the games I had seen on the television. Once my father took me to a hall. There was a long table covered in a white cloth, tiny wicker bowls lined with napkins and filled with candy, chips, nuts; plates of hot food and a soda fountain. This wasn't a children's party. In fact, there were not many children there, just me and my sisters. Music played and the adults danced. I watching them thump around the middle of a room, clunky bodies rattling like loose change. When my father danced, he would hunch his shoulders down and bend his left knee inward and click, his neck cocked to the side. He liked to throw out sharp winks to any woman who dared to look. He grabbed the waist of some blonde woman and pulled her close. I saw his hand on her hip. It gave me a sudden feeling: No, I want to dance with dad. But he wouldn't let me, I stand on his toes, he wants to dance with Tracey, go and sit with your sisters and watch. A thorny wave foams out of my chest. I sulk for the rest of the evening.

He is afraid of robbery, somebody might invade our home one day. Keep the windows locked, the doors bolted, the curtains drawn—what if someone came inside and kidnapped you? "If anybody tries to snatch you from your bed when you are sleeping, just scream! I'll come."

"You know what you say if you get snatched: *fire!* Nobody will come to you if you yell 'help'."

"You know what they do to little girls, don't you? Stay out of those toilet blocks, are you fucking stupid? Anybody could come in there and take you. You wouldn't be my daughter anymore! You would be gone!"

He grabs the handle of the door and twists it, back and

forth, is it locked? Up and down, over and over. Sometimes it takes five minutes, he has to be sure the door is locked. He goes around the house and checks the other handles, yes, those are locked too. But is the other door locked? What about the window? Twenty minutes, he isn't ready yet. I forget to lock the door one day. I don't really care anyway, maybe it would be fun if somebody invaded the home. He screams at me, opening and slamming the door over and over "You (slam) always (slam) lock (slam) the door (slam!)".

I like the crazed look on my dad's face when we swear. But if we don't run quick enough he grabs our throats and forces our mouths open with his fat fingers. His nails are dirty, bitter in my mouth. He drags a wet bar of soap across our tongue. My sisters vomit over his shoes. He doesn't stop. He keeps jamming the soap in, washing out our mouths, rinsing them of the filth. This will make us good people, you know. He makes us swallow the salty soap, he doesn't let go until we ingest it and the floor is covered in chunks of soapy, orange mire.

What is it like to kiss somebody? I have seen it done, how people throw their faces together and press close. Why would they do that?

I find out.

My father kisses me goodnight, but doesn't pull away.

How did he know I wanted to see what it felt like?

He holds his face close, I see his eyes—they are wide, open, popping out of his head. What is he doing, I can't pull back? He sucks on my mouth, his tongue pushes up against mine. Is this what it's like to kiss? It's dark in my room, he is meant to be putting me to sleep—tucking me in and reading a story. Tonight he is kissing me and now I know what it is to be kissed. I forget about this happening, I think maybe it was me who did it because I was curious to know. But I didn't put my tongue in his mouth. Logic is of no use here, nothing makes sense to me anymore. When friends say to me, "Who was your first kiss?", I cannot tell them it was my father.

My father drives me to school sometimes. We never leave right away. He likes to sit in the car and stare at my legs. We don't drive anywhere for five minutes. My mother comes out, "What are you doing? Is something wrong with the car?" I don't look at him when he stares, I sit and float into a space where I have no legs, no arms, no body. I forget about my body until I get to school and classes start. 9.30am and my bowels open up, my stomach clenches, a wildfire tears through my flesh. I soak the toilet in my rot all morning. Yes—my body tells me—you are alive, you cannot escape yourself for long. This happens every day when he drives me to school, when he tucks me in, when he kisses me good night, when he wakes me up. He's my father, he loves me.

He helps me over a fence. We are playing a game with a ball, throwing it to each other as hard as we can. It disappears into the neighbour's yard. The fence is only small, perhaps a metre high. We live next to a paddock with a horse and some dirty white sheep that make too much noise. He hauls me over to find my ball. I look up and see the horse grazing on grass nearby. He lifts me, his hand grips between my legs.

"Can't he just pick me up under my arm?"

But he doesn't. He holds his hands there, pressed tightly into my genitals. I squirm a little, but he doesn't let go.

I forget where I am, I disappear for a long time, I don't live in my body anymore, it's down on the ground. I float like an alien, up into my space ship. My mother comes home and sees what my father has done. She has been shopping with my sisters and brother. They stare at me, at my father.

They have all seen what he has done. My mother tells us all to leave, to go play.

"I need to talk to your father."

My father likes to urinate in front of us, he likes it when we see. He pretends to be angry, but he turns his whole body so that he stands in front of us—arms shaking because he is angry, his penis flopping out of his pants. My sisters and I just stare, how can we look away from this sight? He zips up his pants and I see his penis sticking out, straight and stiff. He walks around in front of us, "I'm sorry for being angry, can I have a hug?"

My sisters and I laugh, "What is that thing coming out of your body!" Our laughter cuts through him, he is angry again. The flagpole disappears.

My stomach is always on fire. I clutch the blanket, I hold myself in the shower, I want to curl up when I sit in the car. I claw at my genitals. I hate that it wants me to feel something, that it wants to be touched. When I get to school in the morning, I have to be myself. My friends are giggling, smelling each other. Their hair is long, straightened. They wear perfume and mascara. My hair is tainted, streaked with olive oil, scalp encrusted with cornflakes.

But I have to relax here; I have to learn. I like maths—I am good at solving equations—the best in the class. I am the fastest at calculus. "I have never seen anybody do it that fast. I can't even do it that fast!" my teacher says. But I can't keep solving the problems; my body releases its toxic energy when I start to think.

I have to shit. It is a horrible, nervous river of fetid milk. I am in the toilet every morning for almost an hour. I sit on the toilet and pull and pick at my oily, rank hair. My fingers are greasy and calloused. My face is stained with red and blocked pores. I get upset when people laugh at me, when they poke fun because I spend so long in the toilet. I want to tell them, "well maybe if *you* spent the morning having *your* father stare and grope at your legs then you would be in the toilet too". This thought is so clear in my mind, I am repulsed by it. That can't be true, I think. That's not what is happening. Fathers love their children. Families are good. I close my eyes. I think about jumping. I heard some people do it off bridges.

LIE ALGEBRA

I wait for my body to change. I learn I have a hole, I didn't know I had a hole, but there is a cavity deep inside me and it will begin to bleed. A baby will come from there; you can put a penis in there; it will bleed; it will smell; there might be pain.

"You will get your period soon."

I will need to wash more frequently, will need to carry spare underwear, will have to be alert to the dormant volcano inside me.

"Where does the blood go when I shower?"

"Down the drain."

I never knew I had a hole. I couldn't feel it, it didn't sing to me like my clitoris did. I didn't know my clitoris was a clitoris either—I called it my beep. Beep would throb all the time; it annoyed me that I couldn't restrain its thunder. When it throbbed, I would think, "beep". Every time it signalled to me, I would have to respond—"Yes, I know"—just to keep up a conscious effort to manage it. If it kept going, I would scream, in my mind, begging it to stop—sometimes I would pound at it with my fist until it turned blue. But it kept up its game, its filthy little dance. I liked to push it against the edge of my bed when nobody was looking, especially when I was running late for school. I would run back inside and grate my hips against the bed post. Was this a naughty thing to do? There is a hole there, somewhere below my beep. I'm too scared to find it, afraid it might grab hold of my hand and soil it. I don't want a foul hand. I don't want it to smell.

I don't want to know that I can go inside myself.

My mother keeps asking if the blood has come. If it doesn't arrive by the time I turn sixteen, she will take me to the doctor. "I'll take you, don't worry." She seems to anticipate it never arriving—perhaps she doesn't want it to arrive. I make her take me shopping for bras. I'm ashamed to change in front of my friends without covering my chest; my breasts are growing, there is fat there now. My nipples keep getting bigger.

"I wonder if I can feed a baby?"

My back is covered in dark, red acne. White satin against red, flaky skin. I am becoming a woman. I don't feel like a woman; I feel like I am living inside some crazed cadaver. My hair is long, thick, fluffy. I hardly ever wash it, it starts to turn into a dank swamp. Crusts of skin and scabs fall out, dandruff covers my pillow. I itch and itch, my beep keeps throbbing—I want to stop itching. I suppose I will have to wash more now. Dad doesn't like to take me out unless I wash my hair, he yells when I itch. His car seat is covered in my dead skin and dried mucous.

It comes before gymnastics class. I change into my leotard and notice my underwear soaked in brown, lumpy goo. Have I defecated without knowing it? It doesn't smell like that. It smells musty, like my grandmother's pantry. I ignore it and perform my routine anyway, there wasn't enough to soak through to the other side. I forget the lumps until later that evening.

"What colour is menstrual blood?" I ask my mother.

"Pink," she replies.

How pretty.

"Well, mine is brown."

"Oh ... yes. That's the dead tissue."

It keeps coming, but stops for no attributable reason. Why has it stopped so suddenly? Am I pregnant? I don't even know any other boys, other than my brother and his friends, who all smell of curried egg. I have never even touched the skin of another boy. I tell mum, she asks if I have been up to any funny business. Of course I haven't, but I think I would like to try. She wonders, "should I take you to the doctor?" She always wants to take me to the doctor. The blood starts soon again. It flows and soils my underwear. I see the same brown stain on the underwear of friends, my mother's large briefs are soaked in brown. My sisters' underwear isn't stained yet—but I think it will be soon enough. We are all covered in brown goo, all the time. Where was the pink my mother spoke of?

I don't have the courage to feel around to see where the blood comes from. That hole, it's too far away from the beep. Should I try to see what it feels like inside there? No. I can't do it. I wear pads and feel like a baby. Out of control, wearing a soiled nappy. I want to slip a finger inside myself. It is hot, dry. I want to swim, I need to try to use a tampon. This is shit.

I try to see how I look inside. When I bleed, it dries in my pubic hair and seals my lips together. I am so bloody. It runs all up my ass, all over my thighs. If I bleed, I stink. Do they know I am bleeding? Can they see the bulge in my pocket from the fresh pad to change into at lunch? I'm a baby again, soiling myself. The pad rubs against the inside of my crotch, large sores grow between my thighs. I get a rash all the time; knotted fur grows out of thick pubic skin. There's a moon between my legs, but I don't want to look at it. I don't want to see those craters, full, beaming, waiting for me to look at them.

I can't stand it any longer, I want to swim, run, wear a dress and not worry about that soggy nappy hanging between my legs. I hold the edge of the bathroom sink and place a mirror underneath my groin. I see blood, twisted flesh, masses of hair. What the fuck is this alien between my legs? I can't really see a hole, I see folds of skin, looping into each other. It smiles at me, my lips are smiling to say hello. I see it throb when I touch it, "It moves!" How strange to watch it do that. I open my lips with two fingers, fresh brown lumps have stuck to the edge of pink flesh, it makes a wet pop. I edge my finger closer to where I think the hole is. It seems too far away from where I have been before, am I going to end up in my asshole? That thought disturbs me even more than my bloody vagina.

Pink lips hang over white, hairy skin. They never used to be there, they used to be tucked inside, neat and tidy. I am a woman now.

I take the tampon, white, wrapped in plastic, and remove it carefully. I shouldn't handle it too much—it might make me sick to put something dirty inside—the hole is delicate, fragile, prone to infection. The wrapper warns that this tampon might kill me; I must take it out after four hours. So I hold it delicately by the edge, by the tips of my fingers. Still crouching, I push. The tampon won't budge through. I push harder still and feel a fire running through my lips. The pain is furious, my hole screams "No! Not big enough". My hymen is still intact, but I have to push through the sacred lining to keep clean and stop the blood flowing. No nun ever told me that my hymen is going to get in the way of this tampon. Fuck my body.

Why should this rotten brown blood show that I have become a woman? Dead egg, dead cells, stinking, heaving, wretched thing. I love the blood now, of course. I have become fond of it. I know when it is coming. I start to press my legs together, my lips full, breasts swell. Ready for baby? What a stupid idea, I'm ready to come, to swim in a pool of my blood and be swaddled by my inflated body. The day before I first got my period, I was playing with the neighbour's cat. He was a beautiful beast, tortoise shell fur, long, elegant—more powerful than me. He rubbed his head against my thigh, purring, his tail licked the curve of my ankle. Perhaps someone might know that I am alone here with this cat, come remove the clothes from my body, press up hard against me and relieve this fireball inside my lap. I straddle a chair, it feels good. I want the cat to do it—what if I sit with my legs open. Will he fall into me? He doesn't. I feel guilty sitting on the floor—legs spread wide open—silently begging a cat to fuck me.

I fall in love with the world, with the sun over my pale legs, the jasmine along the fence, the bus driver who hands me my ticket—what if I lean in just a little bit closer to you, put my hand down your jeans, you see how I want to be touched. No, puberty does not begin with dead blood. It began when I saw my friend Amelia quietly slip her shirt over her head, tanned back, black bra, slender arms reaching for a hairbrush. The sudden curve of her hip, it never used to be like that. That is becoming woman. My older cousin Hallie gives me a kiss hello; she looks like Snow White, long dark hair, pale skin, crisp breath, sultry, her puffy breasts push against my body as she leans in. Her lips were pink, alive, marshmallows touching my cheek. I shrink away from her, surprised at how this kiss makes me feel, how quickly I succumb to the blood rushing to fill the crater between my legs.

I think she knows, too.

How the blood can make you feel alive! How you will want to rub your crotch against the headboard of your bed over and over. When I push down my underwear, I see how I am becoming woman. A thick string of yellow mucous caught in the cotton mesh refuses to detach from my lips. As it hardens and dries it grabs onto long pubic hair and pulls tightly, trying to force the hair out of my skin. The yellow would dry out in the crotch of my underwear and make a chalky paste. Mix it with the brown goo and make a woman. What a messy thing my hole has become.

I obsess over my vagina. Is it bleeding, is it making more of that yellow stuff? I squish my legs together, back-and-forth, wanting to see where I could take my body. What does it feel like to orgasm? Open, shut them—making cleavage, opening my legs. I watched the changes in my body like watching an automatic door. But I couldn't see what I looked like in the mirror. I didn't see who I was, how my awkward gait and oily skin signalled my naïveté and innocence, and how I craved to be touched. They would cat-call in the street, honk their horns, frighten and seduce me. I would return home and lie in bed, letting my hand wander underneath my skirt, wondering what would happen if they pulled their cars over to the side of the road, let me sit in their car, push open my legs, straddle me. Wrapped up in my doona, warm from the air that blew out of the duct above me, I think about what it would feel like to share a bed.

How am I going to learn about these desires I feel? I think about my fear of Satan, how afraid I used to be that he could take my soul. The melody my body sings is too loud now, I am not so afraid of Satan anymore. But I am afraid of Jesus, He seems more powerful. He's not going to eat my soul, but I know that he watches me closely, listening, knowing everything that I do. I don't want to be looked at all the time, I don't want everybody to know what I am doing—but they do know—they know exactly what I am doing at every second of the day. I admit, I stare at people, their breasts, the bulge between their legs, arms, legs, hands, ears, nose, eyes. Where do their hands go, what do their fingers do? What are thinking when they take a shit?

We caress each other's hair in class. That feels good, that feels like what I imagine sex will feel like. I have never seen a boy's penis, but I dream about them. I dream about the ugly boy I let kiss me, he smelt strange, but I let him do it anyway. His tongue pushes between my lips, darting around my mouth, tunnelling toward the edge of my throat. He makes me gag, but I have never been held in this way. I push him off me, this is not the right thing to do, but my beep is screaming for more, I think about what he might want to do to me. That night, I dream about being locked inside a prison. In the prison dream, he opens his fly—I cannot make out what is there—but he pushes me down against the floor, his tongue inside my mouth like before. The concrete floor feels hard against my hips; he thrusts against me. I wake up. It feels like I'm floating.

* * *

We take a train to visit the city police station. I get to sit next to the police officer accompanying the class. A man boards the train. He is middle aged, scruffy, his eyes and mouth twisted together—perhaps from years of drinking. He feels his youth, he still wants to be attractive; his jeans are so tight I see a lump between his legs. I cannot look away— even though I am sitting next to the police officer—the bulge is too bright. What is beneath that thick, blue cloth?

He sees me staring. He winks and smiles. He has caught the attention of a twelve-year-old-girl who knows nothing more than the fire between her legs and the hole in her head. I want him to take me away from the train, take off my clothes and show me the force of my body.

I masturbate furiously. I have not figured out how to climax. I suppose I have gotten the technique confused with what I understand about male anatomy. I think it needs to be rough, violent, exposed, bloody. I lie down on the lounge room floor and rub myself until it hurts. I pound at the tiny spot on my body, it throbs back at me screaming "Not enough!" A cruel trick this body has played, why can't I know how to make it feel good? I do not yet know that my orgasm will be like the blood I shed every month, a slow trickle gliding over the edge, bubbling fountain, sluggish foam.

I am stifled by the world in which I exist. But, in truth, it probably wouldn't have mattered if I lived in the electric bustle of the big city or out in some dirty shack, I would have always suffered from the pain of my hole. Still, how can I stimulate myself in these feigned badlands: concrete desert, windy bus terminal, ridiculous bike trails; insincere hallways that lead to nowhere but more of the same. I have no mirror, no place to discharge this pent up energy, my sexual, intellectual, emotional energy forced into a box of capitalist cinema, all-you-can-eat restaurants and an education concerned with the rules of netball, topographic maps and recipes for sherbet. A world where history, mathematics, languages, science, philosophy are lost because they have no product. "We do not study philosophy here, Larissa, it is not a pre-requisite for entry to university." "You only need to study Japanese for two hours per week, that is surely enough!" "Sorry, Larissa, we don't study films at this school—only books".

Lost on an infinite plateau, circling through the same emotions and intensities. Perhaps this is how people develop schizophrenia? I feel I might be schizophrenic. Sometimes I enter into an eccentric trance, some spontaneous hiccup that I can't control. All my thoughts and feelings become moderated through a hyperbolic witch who forces the volume and content of my thoughts into overdrive. My brain submerges itself in battery acid, my impulses turn to sludge, and I am at the command of the witch. My neck feels heavy when I enter this phase, the witch cackles at me. My thoughts are so loud, my fingernails try to tear themselves away. I see a tree, I know it's a tree—but I feel confused. I sit and stare at it, what is this thing growing up from the dirt? I find a web of dead skin caught beneath my heel and pull back, watching it slice away until it drops.

* * *

I have to take the bus home and walk the rest of the way every afternoon. Ninety minutes of travel along windy roads that lead to nowhere. When I travelled to Italy on a school trip, I was surprised by the signs that pointed to foreign lands, a train that weaved through Germany, Holland, Belgium, France—a highway you could follow all the way to Asia. It was so disorienting, I could not speak the language well, the food was different, the toilets too close to the floor. I sat by myself most of the journey, too anxious to do anything else. On this afternoon, my bus only takes me to my housing estate, past a graffitied wall, a strip of grass covered in weeds, an abandoned petrol station. My backpack pulls on my neck, forcing me backwards. I heave along this hellish tunnel, dragging my body back to that cave of bland dinner, scheduled programming, a drunken mother, oil heaters, homework.

My uniform is heavy. Our skirts have to be long, our shirts tucked in, buttons done up, blazers adorned. My shoes must be formal, chunky, hard. I must wear this every day or I will have to stay back after school. They will keep me there even longer. I wear two pairs of underwear, afraid somebody might see the blood-soaked pad through my thin grey skirt. It rubs inside my thigh and gives me giant blisters. We have to line up and have our uniforms checked regularly, making sure hems are long, nails are clean, ears and tongues free of metal. My mother ensures that I am enrolled in a school that forbids open interaction with the opposite sex, forbids anything but study for university and religious instruction. I am watched constantly by parents and teachers, they are afraid I might open myself up. I am not ready for that, I am too young to know how to feel pleasure without consequence. My virginity must be preserved. If you lose it, you will regret that for the rest of your life. If you fall pregnant and have an abortion, you will regret that for the rest of your life. My hole is a dangerous place. They know about what it wants, how I am some rampant, crazed, wretched volcano waiting for some lucky mirror-man to come press the switch and unleash the lava. Not yet, they say, wait. If you wait, you will go to heaven. If you don't wait, Jesus will know about your lustful thoughts and you will be miserable forever. I don't believe them, but sometimes I do.

I can no longer stand to sit in this place. I have become catatonic, a slave to the dead skin on my foot. I pick at it constantly, watching the yellow peel from the pink. My foot is like a peach, what soft flesh lies beneath? I wish I could see the veins that run along the side, long hoses that lead all the way to my heart—but it hurts too much to pull the skin back from there. I have to stop, my foot should not be so interesting to me. I find a train timetable and walk my body to the station. Where I am going—I don't know. I stare out the window of my train and watch yellow grass change into ramshackle terrace houses, trams, mysterious shops. I let the train carry me right into the city, into the place of green gardens, black espresso, record stores. I find a park and dump my body there for nearly six hours, watching people walk by, staring at the trees in front of me. I write poems and sketch the ducks that waddle past. My mind is blank, empty, a void. I have trouble closing my mouth, the nape of my neck feels heavy, it seems to be holding gallons of fluid. I find a cinema called *Lumiere*. The theatre is tiny and seats only a few dozen. I can hear the projector whirring behind me, a beacon of light streaks through the dark air—a new world opens up in front of me. Strange to see people so deeply engaged in conversation, to see women touching other women, questions provoked, children openly dissatisfied. This cinema makes me feel lethargic. It gives me too much information.

* * *

My father buys a computer because my brother needs the Internet for school. What is this new window? I am quickly transfixed and learn how to navigate through the new machine. I create an avatar and find places where people talk about more than blood, pain and the trauma of a ripped hymen. They send me secret messages, telling me about what they want to do to my body. I create dozens of emails, I say I am a boy, a woman, a seventeen year old, I'm twenty-five. I'm really twelve. I never look the same, change my photograph often, create new names. I want to live in California, Kansas, London, Montréal. One man chats to me often, he adds me on ICQ. He tells me he has a wife, but no children. Have I ever been to a nightclub? He is a DJ, but doesn't take drugs—he doesn't need to, the music keeps him alert, he feels as though he lives in a different body when he plays. Would I like to go with him? What am I doing? Am I touching myself?

Yes.

I had to lie—the computer was close to the living room, my mother was drunk on the couch and would occasionally call out to me. I obviously don't want to touch myself in her presence. I will do that later—in private. Where is the pink, do you look at yourself, what do you taste like, have you ever had sex? So many questions, I create answers. When I am home alone, I shift my legs across the edge of the chair and roll my underwear over the swollen folds of skin. It is wet in there—it looks different. My lips are full, they move with a pulse.

I tell a woman I have never had an orgasm, so she writes a long passage to me, describing how to open your legs underneath a tap and let warm water flow over yourself. She says that my body will burst open if I do that. "It must be concentrated", she writes, "best to do it in the bath". I try it, pushing my pelvis to the edge of the hard, blue bath, hoisting my legs over the edge, gripping my backside with two hands. I must look ridiculous, perched so peculiarly like this. It is an awkward position, difficult to hold myself in for a long time. I open the tap and watch the water gush over my legs. The water rises up from the bottom of the bath and envelopes across my skin. My vagina sputters, it starts to clench uncontrollably. I nearly jolt back at the sudden reaction, how is it possible that this soft water has caused me to shake so violently? Quickly, I am succumbed to some strange new sensation, my lips, tongue, the soles of my feet centre now on my cunt, these two fatty lips become my everything. I start to bathe like this every night of the week.

* * *

Soon after its purchase, the computer becomes the sacred object, the centre of our passion. We all stop going to church because dad is too tired after being up on the computer all night. It is rarely turned off, almost always occupied by somebody—it becomes difficult to grab a moment alone on the machine without disturbance. My sisters like to play simulation games, pretending to care for a cat—the aim is to feed, pet, preen the virtual creature, as they do to their pets outside, making sure that the virtual animal is always happy. My brother likes to read about football and look at pictures of American film actresses. My father looks at porn. My mother does not know how to operate the computer; she does not even know how to turn it on. My father demanded to be left alone when he looked at porn. Usually he would make use of the computer in the early hours of the morning when everybody was asleep—but sometimes he could not help himself, and would retreat to the study quickly after dinner. If we tried to talk to him during this time, he would scream and—in a panic—try to shut down the window before we could see what he was looking at.

My brother liked to sneak up behind me to see what I was doing. He had become obsessed with my changing body. He walked in on me in the shower, in the bedroom when I was changing, whenever I was naked. He would open the door quite suddenly and without knocking, entering the bedroom or bathroom only to stand and stare at me. He wouldn't leave, even if I started screaming. He had many questions for me: How does it feel to have a period? Do you wear a bra? He saw a receipt in my mother's purse after a doctor had to examine my vagina: "What did they do to you?" He smiled when he asked me. He met a girl at his job stacking supermarket shelves; she worked on the checkout, she also did gymnastics, but she was older. "Her routines are sexier" he tells me. "You should dance like her, thrust your hips like this, see, forward."

He liked to watch me do the splits. I wished I could lock the bathroom, but it broke after my brother slammed the door and my father was too busy to fix it. He came into the bathroom once with my brother when I was showering, and neither would leave. They stared at me, laughing while I screamed—desperately throwing soap, towels, whatever I could find at them without moving my free hand that covered my body—until my mother finally managed to haul herself out of bed and stop the excitement that I had created with my cries. "What a silly girl you are." My father just laughed at me and claimed he was fixing the tap.

My brother sneaked up behind me and read the conversation I was having with a stranger. He sees what I have written, how I tell this stranger what I want done to my body, what I want to do to his. He yells, excitedly, for my father to come into the room.

I don't even know how to describe the anger I saw inside my dad. Even what I did with Sabine did not make him this angry. He looks confused, crazed, like when my mother told him I had my period and asked him to run down the street and buy sanitary napkins. He reads the transcript aloud, and I immediately see that I have cut a deep hole in him. He steps back from the monitor and grabs a fistful of wires, ripping the modem out of the wall. There is a violent flash of electricity, plaster shatters everywhere, chips of white snow fall all over the room, drifting silently over the computer keyboard.

He makes me recall what I had written three times over.
"What did you want him to do to you again?"
"Say it again."
"What did you write to that man?"
"How did you want to be treated by this stranger?"
We don't get another modem for years.

* * *

School became a very boring place in my fourteenth year. Writing mock newspaper reports, studying the rules of cricket, what is acidic and what is basic. None of this was terribly interesting to me. I did learn that people used to throw their shit out the window and that because women used to wear so many layers of clothing, they had to piss right into their dress. Otherwise, everything made me indolent. I would regularly feign illness to think quietly in the sick room behind the school office. I liked to lie on the bed and stare up at the ceiling. The room was very bare, three beds were placed side-by-side, a picture of Jesus hung above the door. Jesus would stare back at me; his heart was glowing through his chest. I look at his heart and think how all the veins in my body run back to that organ, an unseen web for circulation. If I stretched my circulatory system out, it would wrap around the earth twice over.

The ceiling was low, I could touch it if I stood up on the bed. It was an old room, rotting wooden pylons ran across the length of the roof. I wonder what would happen if I threw a knotted sheet over that wooden beam, tied the sheet around my neck and jumped off this bed? Would the beam break above me? Surely the railing would support my body if the knot were tight enough? Nobody would see, everyone was busy in the classroom. This blank thought, the ease with which I think about my expiration sends a wave of calm running over me.

* * *

I took gymnastics classes three times a week. But, once I started menstruating, I could no longer stand the touch of my gymnastics teacher. She would hold my legs and stomach to show me how to correct a particular movement, but I would crumble beneath her, unable to focus on anything but her gripping hand. My eyes wandered to the movements of other girls' bodies; the shape of their backsides, the snap when they tugged at their leotards, the precision of their movements. Some of them could flip very high—I was jealous. I had been adept at shifting my centre of gravity, moving my body with the right precision and skill; but the sight of new hair, the feel of a tampon, the scent of my underarms, halted my body in its tracks and I could no longer perform.

I felt limited, confined. I couldn't flip anymore, couldn't dance, my arms and legs shook whenever I tried. I raised both arms above my head, hoping to spring up onto the bars above me, but I couldn't move. My teacher grabbed my backside, firmly squeezing it, growling in my ear: "Get going!"

I couldn't perform for her. There are too many people listening, smelling—they hear the sound of a dead fish writhing in a pool of mud, the smell of its carcass rotting. A dozen girls lift their legs above their heads and twirl for an audience who wants nothing more than to see their lips ripped open, to smell the room filled with the moist air and salted oyster.

I get fitted for a costume. One woman fits everybody's costume. She takes me to the corner of the hall, instructing me to stand with my feet apart, my arms slightly raised, eyes looking straight ahead. She slides her hands over my body, checking to see how this new costume suits. It fits perfectly, there is no problem, but she continues her work quietly, curling her fingers inside the elastic of the leotard, pushing herself inside my genitals. I don't wear underwear with a leotard, you can't because it shows. Nobody wears underwear and she knows this, that beneath the thick Lycra I am nothing but a naked child. "Sorry, I know this makes you feel uncomfortable", she runs her hands over my breasts. Nobody notices, the class continues its routine, "One, two, three, lift!" I watch my friend Emma hoist herself over the uneven bars; she freezes when she catches sight of my twisted face. This woman has taken over my body, she forces herself in me, my fingers knot, knees set like concrete, saliva evaporates and I ache from the pain of wanting to scream as loud as I could. But I can't, she has influence over me. Emma watches, her mouth agape, while the mother glides her hands along the surface of my skin. Emma says nothing, what could a child do when confronted with this spectacle? She lifts the side of the leotard and rubs three fingers over my breast, she cups her hand between my legs and squeezes, whispering into my ear, "Don't worry, it will be over soon". I wait for her to finish. There is nothing I can do but wait.

* * *

I am startled very easily now. Wind pushing branches along the window becomes a burglar breaking in. A hanging pot plant seems to be a head staring back at me. A broken light bulb makes me jump. When it dies and the room goes dark, I automatically think that somebody must have cut the power to stab me in the black night. The bushes outside my window morph and mutate, they look like a face with almond eyes, a tiny mouth, a frail body. I am obsessed by the thought of extraterrestrials abducting my body, of being kidnapped in the night by a stranger, of being snatched out of sight and mutilated by a knife-wielding psychopath. I have trouble sleeping unless I wrap myself completely in blankets, white knuckles gripped onto pink doona, legs stiff, ready to run in case of attack. I notice my sisters start to do the same when they fall asleep. They are growing too, not identically, but with a certain rhythm. One starts to grow thick hair along her legs, the other begins to bleed, their hair turns into the same dank swamp as mine. Their breasts poke out, they refuse to wear anything but oversize sweat shirts and baggy jeans. We wither together, broken flowers, dead leaves, waiting to be trodden on.

I was ashamed of myself in public, when my body was exposed to others. I wanted to retreat to some private corner and tuck my head under my arm to get to know my new smell. I liked to sit with my arms raised over my head and fondle the thin, black hair that grew out of the pit. I injured my ankle after I attempted a vault and was forced to quit gymnastics, my teacher saying, "Your heart has left the gym." I did not mind. I was happy to spend my time in bed with my ankle raised up on a pillow. I could gaze at my body without any distractions now.

* * *

I take the bus home every day. It takes a long time. Ninety minutes through bush and mountain road, factory-lined highways, cold wind and grey sky, until I reach a point where I am close enough to walk. Ninety minutes sitting on the same bus, looking out the same window. I have grown my hair long; it nearly reaches my waist. Hair is a thing of pride amongst my friends, we have to pin it back during classes in case we catch lice. I like to let it down after school, long, dark-blonde, shiny. I take better care of it now, washing it regularly with sweet smelling shampoo and conditioner. I like to sit with a comb and claw out wet tangles in front of the television.

I watch how the hair slumps over my shoulder and falls onto my breast. What a strange thing my hair is. Why would my body decide to produce long, vacant strands of colour on top of my head? Why not a hard shell, a nail to cover the roof of my scalp—why not just leave it as skin? I see a hair separate from the rest of the pack; it is coiled, dark, alone. The hair has odd splits all along its centre, extra hairs growing out from the middle. There are white dots in between every break, the hair forks at the end.

Is this what a split end is?

I have seen commercials for shampoo that promise to fix split ends. I thought they could only be seen under a microscope.

I pull the hair. My scalp tightens when I release it from its plug. The mutant hair is separated from my scalp now, a weird, bent object. I pull it from both ends and the hair shatters, every fragment too weak to hold onto its mother. It scatters across my lap. What is this that my body has grown for me?

I hunch over on the bus and see how the hair grows all over my body. Unnerving patterns of growth, thicker along my calves: hairs that grow in twos and threes, long and thin up my thigh; a dark mass in the centre, strange, coarse hair. Why does it grow here and not in other places? I have a trail that extends from my pubic mound up into my belly button. It's not so thick, but it's there. I lift up my shirt and pluck it in front of the other passengers on the bus. I forget that I must look very strange to everyone else.

The more I look, the more peculiar hairs that I find. Sometimes the hair is perfect, until a tiny fork breaks the smooth shaft in two. I work at catching the stray and peel the hair in two, my eyes fixated on this new spectacle. Other hairs were so broken and fragmented it seemed miraculous that they were even attached to my head at all. The hair might split almost entirely from the root itself, so torn it appeared to be two separate hairs until I discover the secret truth when I pull out the entire hair. I look for those—they are my favourite, a hair with a dirty secret. I was so immersed in my hair that I missed my bus stop. I had to travel an extra two miles home—I ran most of the way—forcing myself to run. I want to lie on the couch and find some more strange hairs to look at.

I can no longer listen to teachers, friends, my parents, anybody; I just want to sit and pick at my hair. My hair is fascinating, a malformation, a peculiarity. I am on a fanatical quest to find the most interesting hair, the best one to stare at and pull. My fingers become calloused, the way I dig my nails into the soft pad of my fingertips to break the hair from its split hardens them. My neck and back ache because I hunch for hours and hours. I struggle to focus in class, I cannot keep up in conversation, I hardly pay attention when I am talking on the phone—I cradle the receiver under my shoulder and pull on my hairs with a free hand. I start to lose my vision, hours of focusing on tiny fragments of hair ruin my eyes. I need glasses. I can hardly read a book without straining. I sit on the couch every afternoon, every morning, all weekend, and pluck at my hairs. Anything I try to do leads my eyes back to the hairs resting across my chest. I drift in and out of the visual kaleidoscope of broken hairs—my surroundings evaporate, I hear nothing, see nothing, do nothing but immerse myself in this archaeological dig for strange hairs.

What is the most mutant object that my body can make for me?

Hairs start growing increasingly darker on certain points on my body. A thick nest of hair behind my thigh catches my attention. Underneath my calf, I find a group of three hairs that are darker than the rest. I stare at them. They stare back. Were they trying to tell me something, these black hairs? Swimming at the beach, pushing my body through the waves, I stand up and let salt water run down the length of my body. I watch it run across new curves underneath my bathing suit. My heavy stomach, fatty chest, swollen feet. I watch it run over the edge of my thigh and nearly collapse. Long, dark hairs have grown like a forest there. My stomach crumbles and I shrink into the water.

I was so carefree in the ocean, I had forgotten about the presentation of my body—but what if other people had seen such a jungle lurking out from under the elastic? I hunch over when I leave the water, afraid somebody might see the dark hairs that ridicule me. I sit on the hot sand and cover myself legs and torso with a towel, embarrassed, but unable to drag my eyes away from this new-found colony. My fingers stray to my upper thigh and start to pull at the hairs, one by one, under the little tent I make in the towel so that no one else can see. On the beach in the middle of summer, surrounded by tanned, long-legged teenage girls running in the sand, I sit and pluck the hairs out of my thigh.

I try to shave, wax and use depilatory creams. The hairs keep coming back. Why would my body taunt me in this way—if I lost an eye, it would not grow again. My mother had tried to insist that I did not need to shave. When I held up an arm to show how thick hair was growing out of my armpit, she maintained, through her drunken stupor, that she could not see anything. Spit came out of her mouth when she spoke to me on this occasion, and she tried desperately to persuade me that I was still a girl, all the while thick, wine-soaked mucous rained over her precious champagne carpet. She would not buy me razors, not until I was eighteen. I use hers anyway. I prop my legs up on my mother's bed and glide the rusted razor across my leg, watching black hairs fall onto my ankle and drop over her bedspread. When I shaved, it produced a dark rash. A thick line marked where I sheared the razor over my skin, a red highway through black stubble and missed weeds. I was unaware of the need for water and cream, thinking that a razor alone would suffice. The sight of my red legs coated in black stubble, thick, flaky acne across my back, frizzed hair, a half bald scalp, taunted me. This is not becoming woman; this is becoming monster.

* * *

Summer was spent almost entirely at the beach. Hot afternoons were easily passed running in and out of the giant waves the moon pulled along for us. My brother and I frolicked until the sun sank beneath the sky, the water turned liquid navy and the sand went cool. Back and forth between the sea and the sand, sometimes lazing on the yellow shore, watching tiny grains run through my fingers—other times flopping my body onto the top of the water and letting the force of the ocean knock me around down to the sea floor and back up again. When I returned home one evening and finally removed my bathers, I felt impossibly itchy. "Have I been stung by a jellyfish?" Surely this could not happen between my legs—my vagina seemed to be coated in a thin strip of wax, I could not stop rubbing it. The burning continued until the next day, but I ignored it, hoping that it would eventually go away.

In the days following, my vagina began to expel a far thicker discharge than what I was accustomed to. The smell was outrageous, intensely fishy. When I scratched at my genital lips, the thick fluid would soak through my underwear and into whatever pants I was wearing. It looked as though I had urinated all over myself, the yellow gack so thick that it coated my pubic hair, glued to my rectum and caused a rash that ran all over my thighs, up between my legs and all across my pubic mound. I let it persist, unable to stop scratching myself until the fluid saturated and ruined my clothing. I would sit on the couch watching television, my drunken mother by my side, and I would jump suddenly up out of my seat, startled as though I had been stung with a cattle rod. Itching ferociously in front of her, clawing at my genitals with utter desperation, she took no notice and I did not bother to tell her something was wrong. Weeks passed. I began to have trouble urinating, the pain of passing waste so great that I had to immerse my body in a warm bath to soothe the flow.

I could no longer walk. I would have to repeatedly stop and itch; after perhaps five or ten minutes, my genitals, legs and clothing became so completely soaked in the cheesy discharge that I would be forced to return to my room and change my clothing. I contemplated using tampons to soak up the thick cream, but I thought this would probably produce only more pain. I let it pass, enduring a rotten burning when defecating, some impossibility in taking a piss and the pungent smell I emitted from my festering cavity. Perhaps four or five weeks later, it finally became too much and I told my mother.

How she did not realise something was gravely wrong with her daughter, I can only attribute to the fact of her drinking. She was surprised to learn of my predicament and offered to drive me to the doctor the next day, who was promptly startled at the sight of my inflamed genitals. "My goodness, you must be in tremendous pain!"

She ordered whopping doses of anti-fungal medication, and wondered out loud how it was possible that I was able to even walk. I was, of course, suffering from a very bad case of thrush—a condition of which I had not heard at the time. So easily was I able to deny the messages from my body. What I had suffered from for nearly five weeks took another month to get rid of, my mother explaining to my grandmother and teachers that I could not attend school or leave the confines of my bed due to a 'bladder infection'.

Soon after, I decided that my mother was a hopeless cause, lost to cigarettes and alcohol and a youth driven by unquestioning acceptance of dreams for fusion with a husband. When she asked if I needed tampons or sanitary napkins, she could not bring herself to use the correct words, pulling me aside and nervously whispering, "Did you need thingies?" Likewise, she could not bear to even write 'tampons' on the shopping list, choosing to list only scribble a tiny red or blue 'X', red meaning tampons for heavy flow, blue for regular. I would cross it out and boldly write tampons in red permanent marker—an act that usually saw her start a new shopping list without comment.

I refused to talk to my mother—I could not take her advice seriously. What did she know of the world? She had her formal lounge suite; her special wine glasses; half burnt lamb chops, soggy salad; a husband obsessed with porn who talks to her like she was his pet dog. I ask her about what happened when she was a girl, what she wanted to be when she grew up. She told me how she left school, how she worked as a secretary, how she met my father and fell in love. How she wanted a baby. I think, "I never want to be like her. Ever". But I was bound up with her, bound by permission slips, telephone conversations, her driver's license, her money, the roof she provided. Heavy from the quicksand of my predicament, I can't leave—I am her daughter.

We try to bond, to be like a mother and daughter should. She takes me shopping. We don't have much money but we go anyway. She tries to pick out clothes for me, usually pastel dresses that would make me look eighty years old, or floral one-piece swim suits with flesh coloured bras built in, the kind favoured by elderly women. I refuse to buy bathers. I didn't particularly want to go swimming with all the strange new hair, that previous case of thrush, and the fact that my father could not stop groping my body with his eyes. She wants to share a milkshake. When she asks, she sounds like a teenage girl—high-pitched voice, lanky smile strewn across her face. I think she wants the two of us to suck chocolate sludge through straws and giggle about boys. I don't want to talk about boys with her, about my split ends, my beep, those Internet conversations. My mother tells me how she thinks I will make a good teacher, a good librarian, maybe even a nurse. I don't want to share a milkshake with her, disgusting sweet syrup sloshing in our stomachs. I come from her fluid, I am made by her, we share the same blood— why add chocolate milk on top of that mix?

Perhaps it was the lack of oxygen in the mall or its harsh fluorescent lights, but I am suddenly overcome by a migraine and vomit all over the shiny, tiled floor.

* * *

In the beginning, my mother started drinking after dinner. As time went on, it became as soon as she got home from work—though I never saw her drink much before 4pm. She was good at that, at keeping her secret. I hear her say to friends how she just needed a drink to "digest her meal" and to "relax". I never want to have to use something so disgusting to make myself feel relaxed. She usually drinks while watching movies, the kind with a happy ending. I watch her cry when the movie ends, then she rewinds to the start and watches it over again. Sometimes she does this many times in a row. It carries on for months: the same movie, the same story, the same seat on her clean couch. She loves it when they play music in the film, when everything gets gushy and the man leans in to kiss the woman. She loves that, to hear "My Heart Will Go On" by Céline Dion when they fall in love. She watches that scene ten times over.

She vacuums often. She is frantic about keeping the carpets and couches clean. These are the centrepieces to her home, where she likes to sit and drink. She vacuums early on Saturday mornings, when I am trying to study, when we are watching a movie. She makes us move our feet—the television flickers from the electrical interference—and yells at us for not helping. We never help enough with her cleaning. She vacuums when she wakes up at 4am, because my father has been on the computer all night. She runs the machine back and forth outside our door, yelling at us for being useless.

She likes to offer me advice when she is drinking. She sits hunched in her easychair; her body littered with salted snack food and spilt red wine from a plastic bladder. Her gas is foul, savoury, heavy, sulphuric; it languishes in the air wherever she is. She wants to know why I never talk to her, why I don't open up to her the way I do to my friends, why don't I help out more around the house? She asks if I am a lesbian, if I like boys. She says she is worried for me, for my future. But then, she tells me how disgusting it is to kiss somebody, how awful it makes you feel. She sounds like a five year old, afraid of boy germs—but she is talking to her sixteen year old daughter. Who is this woman I am sitting next to? I do not feel that she is my mother, how could she be my mother? We are not the same.

My father likes to keep my mother drunk. He likes to take advantage of the specials at the supermarket, buy four casks of wine and get 10% off. He buys clean skins, wine without a label. It is only $2 per bottle. He fills the house with wine—it's under all of our beds, in the cupboards, in his shed, in the computer room. They never run out of wine. Father becomes upset when mother collapses in the hallway, when she passes out on the couch, when she can't open both her eyes at the same time. Sometimes she becomes emotional and breaks the furniture, or bursts into tears when her film turns sad. She doesn't seem to notice that my father is talking to other women on the computer, that he is receiving odd phone calls in the middle of the night. My sisters and I look at his phone a few times. We see the messages from Candy, Trisha, Barb. We call them to see who they are and decide from the strange, paranoid purr of their voices that they must be prostitutes. I decide I need to move out as soon as possible.

CATEGORY THEORY

It is impossible to avoid cultivating love. One has to be devoted to something; however fanatical, prosaic, cliché or colourful this may be, the human disposition will naturally redefine it beneath an undivided banner called *love*. My portal into the new world was opened through the influence of my teachers. Just the ones who wanted their students to see and transform, who liked to make the world an unfamiliar place and keep the possibilities of their pupils open and awake. I didn't always fall in love. There were teachers who were more obsessed with straight lines, lost pens, smudged ink and incorrect answers—I hated those ones quite naturally—just as I hated the ones who exploited my sense of vulnerability. But there were still many to love.

I began to obsessively worship the most intelligent, the most engaged. First, my adorations were only for women, ones who ripped apart everything I thought I knew about the world and made it beautiful. I longed to know the lives inhabited by these creatures, they seemed far more stimulated and alive than me. They ate strange food, saw films in odd theatres in the city, read new books, were filled with weird ideas, had sex. They were nothing like me. I could not desist from filling my brain with fantasies of their lives, constantly wondering what were they doing, what were they eating, what kind of people were they friends with? What were their families like?

My attraction scared me. I became crippled in front of them, barely able to open my mouth. When they spoke my chest would collapse, I couldn't talk without my hands going numb and trembling. I wondered, "Am I a lesbian for falling in love with these women?" How could a person possibly feel so desperately attracted to an adult without something being grossly wrong with their brain? Teachers might be attracted to their students; they should not get too close in case they molest their students. I knew the rules—I knew I was not allowed to be alone with my teachers, to tell them too many secrets, to see them out of school. But that was all I could dream about, leaving my home and running away with them.

She read us the Brontë sisters. I didn't know that women had always felt the same pain, the same thriving desire to burst into the world, but were throttled by the grip of the more powerful: father, husband, brother, mother, grandmother. She read us strange poems about blood, about loneliness, about boredom. I felt desperate in her classes—I could taste and smell the freedom that would come after I graduated—but I was afraid, with no sense of my self, no knowledge of the world, no economic ability to escape my home. I knew it, I knew how naïve and stupid I was, but I couldn't leave on some bus in the middle of the night. I am still a girl: long, spindly legs, unkempt eyebrows, mousy brown hair, unable to open my mouth and have a conversation with the people at whom I marvel the most.

To overcome my fear, I began to demand secret meetings with her. I had fallen in love with her easily. She taught us wild poetry, about what it was like to travel to the Middle East, how to drink coffee without milk or sugar. She agreed to talk with me in private, and seemed to enjoy indulging in the subject of my youth. We sat in secluded classrooms during our lunch hour, hidden away from the screams of the schoolyard. My peers would giggle when I left to see her, wondering out loud about why I would need to talk to her so often. They also thought I was a lesbian. I wanted to tell them the truth. Sometimes my mind would scream at them that my father exposed himself to me, that my mother passed out on the couch every night. But how do you tell your friends that you need a woman to talk to? Their mothers liked their daughters, they don't drown themselves in alcohol and a television set every night. Our conversations were stunted by my nervousness and I offered little to her in the way of revelation. Still, it gave me the possibility for my own voice.

* * *

I started working. $5-an-hour to push groceries through a machine and count change, to smile at customers and wipe down shelves. It felt lonely behind the cashier's desk. I gave regular customers discounts—especially if they had children. I don't know what they thought, seeing the discount at the bottom of their receipt. I only wanted to be their friend. I would dream of joining their family, wondering where they went to after this shopping. The customers stopped coming to my counter, perhaps afraid I would get into trouble. Or perhaps they sensed the uneasy loneliness, the desperation in my eyes when I pushed the button to lessen the total.

I hardly spent any of my money. I was too scared to shop in the youthful stores. Shopping was a startling initiation ceremony into the world. Totally unreal: for sexually-empowered, physically-aware and attractive bodies only. The weight of pulsating music, provocative storefronts, tight jeans and confrontational shop assistants smothered me. Why did they always want to know how I was?

People kiss hello now, they hug and touch each other. They want to know how you are. "How am I?" What a weird question to ask. They smile at me, bright white teeth, orange skin, streaked hair, jeans hugging their peachy backsides.

I couldn't keep walking around looking like a loser. We had a religious seminar with the local boys' school. I was nearly seventeen and this would be the first contact I had with the opposite sex outside of my home. I couldn't traipse around in printed leggings, fleecy sweaters, oversized T-shirts. I find clothes that help, fitted shirts with puffy prints of cartoons emblazoned on the breast. Cute cats, dinosaurs, monkeys. These clothes become my uniform. I colour my hair dark purple to match—not bothering to fix the roots on a regular basis. My underwear, shoes, T-shirts and jeans are adorned with prints of The Smurfs, unicorns, My Little Pony, daisies, Rainbow Brite. My slight frame still had not developed to full feminine capacity. I had no need for a bra. I had piled on weight after stopping gym, but it lingered on my stomach like a child or a man. No hips to show that I was a woman. Fat belly, long limbs: a pregnant horse.

* * *

The chaperoned meeting with the local boys' school was an event that sprouted an eruption of broken hymens. Boys were quickly claimed, new friendships formed—our tiny group of female friends spawned into a giant circus of dozens of youths. Parties shifted from simple girls-only sleepovers to all-night drunken orgies. People passed out, drugs and alcohol became routine, police were called in to break up fights, some girls had to have their stomachs pumped after they drank bottles of vodka. I would gaze at couples interlocking hands, how they squeezed themselves into each others' flesh and spoke so freely about having sex.

When we went swimming, the girls would wrap their legs around their lover's body. I floated by, pretending not to stare at the alien bodies my friends inhabited. I refused to drink or have sex. I was frightened of being like my mother, of losing control of my body like she would, rocking back and forth, eyes half closed, head rolling over the tops of her shoulders. I couldn't kiss anybody, either. I wanted to, of course I did. I told you I masturbated all the time, gripped by the dedicated blood flow my new body had granted my genital organs. But to let somebody else be a part of that, I simply couldn't do it. I knew it was because of my father, that I was consecrated to his agency, possessed by his power. How could I remove myself from being haunted by disgust?

Then—

I was surrounded by a dozen friends, all eagerly watching a spectacle unfold before them. I had become the butt of their jokes, the only one in the group to have the taint of 'never been kissed'. I was seventeen, a baby in cartoon clothing. I lay on the bed, silently listening to a lively exchange occurring between my friends.

"Who wants to be the one to do it?"

A boy had enough of the chatter and he stood up. Silently grinning, he volunteered his services. The room turned quiet. He pushed himself on top of me and shoved his tongue between my closed lips. What a spectacle, a surprised girl's mouth wetted by a boy in the company of a crowd cheering him on. He burrowed a free hand through the grip of my jeans and rubbed and squeezed at my arse—this action only caused the boys to cheer him on even more. Feeling poked at like a pin-cushion, I tell him to stop. I wasn't ready for this yet, that's the line, isn't it: "I'm not ready". He pulled himself off, wiping saliva from his mouth, the crowd hooted and clapped. My friend Caitlin whispered in my ear, "Well done, but I feel sorry for you". He led me outside, away from the jeers and catcalls to continue his game in private. But, even though I felt some arousal from his probing tongue, I couldn't go on. I felt too estranged from my body. I went to bed.

Then—

I finally allowed myself a drink. I was eighteen. Seeing the influence it had over the condition of my friends seemed unlike the reaction it gave my mother. They were happy, jubilant at how the liquid relieved their inhibitions. Drunk for the first time, I retreated to a car with strange boy. We sat in the dark and I let him push his dick inside my mouth. At first I had demanded that he go down on me. I had not experienced this before and was unwilling to immediately submit to his demands. So I lowered my pants and he swooped his tongue across me a couple of times, sticking his fingers inside my damp crotch, quickly insisting that I should suck on him for a while. I relented. Lowering myself before his open fly and stretching my mouth open, I felt his matted hair glue to the gaps between my teeth. Moist skin filled up my airway. He pushed my head down further. It was difficult to breathe in this position. My body was caught in the space between the two car seats, I had to use my arms to steady myself. Wondering where we had disappeared to, the same friends caught sight of my head bobbing up and down through the soft light of the street and crept over to watch. I raised my eyes from his sweaty groin to see a crowd laughing outside the car, wickedly grinning at the sight of our play. Caitlin pulled me out of the car and, in an act of sympathy, put her arm around me, saying I was disgusting, that I shouldn't let a man do that to me. She had a boyfriend for almost two years, having slept with him at fourteen, and she confessed to me on that night that she regretted it. "Best to wait," she said. Waiting means that men will love you.

The lucky man left the party. But his friend called us all over and rang him on speaker-phone, asking about the performance of my first blow-job. He told everyone, much to my feigned delight, that I was quite skilled.

* * *

Caitlin was my best friend. She looked like a peach, wavy hair rounded across the soft folds of her skin. She was unaware of her grace, of the body nature had granted her. When she was ignorant of her form, she flickered with the vivacity of unlimited youth. She had started drinking before I did, but it was me who initiated our fun.

We were drinking whiskey in her room, clumsily mimicking our idea of adolescence with clothes, punk music and glitter eye-shadow. She lay down on the bed across from where I was standing, her lips wet from the gloss she had slicked over them.

"What does that taste like?"

I did not let her answer, instead I pressed my mouth against the soft pillow of her lips and waited for her nervous reaction. To my delight, she thrust her body into mine and our tongues and hands connected with nervous, electric trepidation. I had never felt anything like this. Even the warm wash of water that made me orgasm was not of the same genealogy. It felt like wading in the softness of a still river. We didn't speak when I pulled back, perhaps too nervous to

85

think about aligning ourselves with the category lesbian. We were too proud in our girlish passivity to assert ourselves with what we thought to be an outlandish eccentricity.

I slid my hand under the seam of her T-shirt; it hovered just underneath the curve of her breast. She took in a surprised breath, my gesture confirming that I wanted to do more than just kiss her. I took my other hand and placed it firmly at the top of her thigh. She was wearing her archetypal uniform, blue jeans, fitted T-shirt, coloured sneakers. The thickness of the denim got in the way of my hand, my hand could not so easily be felt, so I impelled myself to press harder, to nudge my fingers just a little more to the left. She had not expected such an embrace, and I felt her groin throb underneath my palm.

We stopped for a while to attempt sleep, a little disturbed by the intensity of our actions. At first we lay on mattresses heaped over her floor, silently staring at each other through the dark. That quiet sentence gave way to all the energy and oppression of our desire, unfastening it like a gushing faucet. We ripped off each other's clothes, she lowered her head and put my breasts in her mouth, suckling on them like a baby. She took her long, manicured finger and slid it into the wet damp between my legs. I felt filled by her gesture, but unsure. Is she inside my vagina? Is this what it feels like to have another inside you? She pushed her groin into my face, but she smelled different to how I expected. Her breath usually tasted of crisp apples; now her skin was musty, more intense. I was not ready to push my tongue into her, though I considered it. We moaned superficially, rolling around her floor, engaged in the pleasure of discovery but still mimicking the actions we thought obligatory. This was my introduction to lived corporeality, and this is what I consider to be the moment I lost my virginity.

For a while, we continued our secret affair—our friends being none-the-wiser. But we eventually stopped after Caitlin found a boyfriend who didn't like the heaviness of my presence. I stopped being friends with Caitlin—and all the crowd of onlookers—soon after I left for university.

FLUID MECHANICS

Graduation came and went and I was never so happy as to see my claustrophobic school be shoved where it belonged: into the past. I moved to the inner city, leaving the staid sack into which I was born. I felt a strange pull to stay, some anxiety from the thought of leaving the only place I had known for my entire life, but the situation at home had become so desperate I had to impel myself to escape. I still felt exposed in the shower, naked to the world even behind the glass screen. My father liked to linger around the toilet; I held onto my childhood belief that he had drilled some kind of peephole to watch me. The inertia in their routine had not changed: my father's random outbursts of anger continued, my mother was always drunk, they still ate the same disgusting meals. My parents helped with the move, following me silently along the highway into the inner suburbs that I would now call home. They carried furniture into my new ramshackle share-house, dumping my possessions coolly in the centre of my bedroom and leaving quickly, preferring to act as removalists rather than parents. I never returned to live with them again.

You probably wouldn't believe how little happened during this time—late adolescence, oneiric youth, immersed in a farce constructed from nothing but the fact that death is a distant mirage far on the horizon. Of course, everything happened in this feigned pinnacle of my existence. I suppose you wouldn't believe how I lived, ate, slept, washed, fucked, worked, all in worship of the social calendar: Thursday, Friday, Saturday, sometimes Sunday or Wednesday—even Monday because beer was $1 on Mondays.

Constipated life—conversation continuously drowned by the pulse of music, faculties dulled from constant intoxication, dreams postponed to continue the cycle of the weekend. My obsession? Sex, of course—we were all obsessed with that. Who was having it, with whom, who diverted their physical attention away from their promised lover— who to exclude from the inner circle of monogamy. If you weren't having it, why weren't you, what was wrong with you? We played incestuous games. We all gradually slept with each other and even created maps that showed how lines connected in a cataclysmic web of rubbed, drunken bodies. This was the mark of the sacred—some determinate force that we defined ourselves by. With whom did we sleep, when, how, where would we do it? So desperate was I to express myself, I ensured my body was always performing. Running naked in public, inserting myself into dark bedrooms at boisterous gatherings and initiating orgies by quietly slipping between the bodies of longstanding lovers. Ensuring that I had slept with everyone so that everyone would know my body.

Casual sex with friends, odd and unscheduled encounters that burst out from the intoxicated night have always been my great vice. Free love sounds good on paper, but in reality most prefer the sanctity of mother—her stability, her warmth, her comfort—a violent body we feign into passivity. My secret truth was my impotence. I never climaxed in any of these brief sessions. The initial power of our interaction, the brief glance, the quick rub, turned masochistic—we slapped our bodies together as though they were plastic dollies imitating real life. I halted myself, reined my body in—a boiled egg, uncracked. Some obstruction stood fast. Perhaps it was my sexual aggression, their guilt from the occasion of their cheating, the fact it took place in unsecure locations. Doubtless these are effects that cannot be ignored—but frankly, this seems all too easy, a counterfeit response. Their languished penises, my persistence, the girlfriends' agonised response seems more the result of an insecure autonomy. I observe the coupling of lovers—their return to infantile language, their fast obsession for each other, the heavy disdain after the split—and compare it to the effect of my strange, fluid encounters, a bond formed by acknowledgement of surface, coquettishly running his hands along the inside of my legs in the shadows of a nightclub, sharing our meals in a restaurant, eyes locking in deep conversation, lazing over each other on the couch. To me, the surrender to spontaneity seems more dynamic, more effectual than a return to the same. I am happier to think of my nebulous affections than the unnerving implosion in tight relationships. Purging all affections onto a singular body seems cool, detached from the fluidity and possibility of interaction.

I do not want to lie to you, but I *have* deceived you in the passage above. I quite naturally crave a continuous supply of warmth and belonging. In fact, it has nearly killed me on several occasions. I write—

Sir—

It is with deepest regret that I confess my condensed nature—it has rendered me a recluse. My desire for you refuses economy. Archaic eruptions, spontaneous combustion, the force of empty satiation, my soul is saturated by your savage presence. How consumed am I with the suggestion that we share this city together, remain connected by hardened concrete, street lamps, the fluctuation of air. The thought that we bathe in this place without intervention renders me catatonic.

I fear my gestures to you are impotent—that my intoxication has subdued my capacity to structure some fluid relation. If nothing else, I am stimulated in the knowledge that the air that sustains us is the same. But this dilutes me; I am nothing without shared compromise. I feel I must destroy myself.

I look at you, you look at me—I create, I lose, I foster a relation that is bound by an obtuse unconscious. I only hope the snatches of space that I feel to be heavy with mutuality are in fact formed by this—not from pure intimation sprung from an isolated self. Otherwise, I am nothing.
—Mlle Bird.

Perhaps it is better to start at the beginning. I will try to explain how I might have found myself in this situation of wildly switching affections. Am I a hedonist or a puritan? My continuing philosophy is to confront my lack. I will attempt to do this for you now.

I was nineteen with an intact hymen, a secret I held onto with some embarrassment. I had slept with many women, of course. After Caitlin I slept with at least five women, but I wanted to try out my body with a man.

Nobody wanted to rip me open. I kept being told that the symbolic act was best left to the man of my dreams. Such a creature did not exist, I knew he was not real—I didn't have any dreams of that nature. But men literally refused my offer, and I sensed that their hesitation came from the fear of my potential for hysteria—that perhaps if they broke me open, I might own them for life. Of course, this is the rationale of an idiot. Nevertheless, I managed to find a man whom I had not known, did not come to know and will never know—his name I cannot recall. I found him in a bar soon after my birthday—I secured his number without confessing that my vagina was still inconveniently in possession of its shield.

I began this process some weeks earlier with quiet anticipation. I wanted to be prepared, ensuring that I had all the right pills and potions to hinder the growth of any foetus or disease within my system. I made an appointment with my physician:

"Have you taken the pill before, do you know how to take it?"

"No."

"Ask your mother. Here's your script."

I suppose the doctor assumed my mother would remember how to take the pill, how it worked and the various interactions it could have with other medications. I suppose she assumed my mother wasn't a drunk who knocked herself out in front of the television night after night. My calm, pretty, suburban appearance must have deceived her into thinking my mother was able to help me. I took the script anyway, finding my own information through the Internet.

Swallowing the tablet produced unexpected results. My body began to take on water, my stomach expanded and it became painful to urinate. My bladder and urethra pushed hard on my pelvis, perhaps trying to escape from the licit drugs I pumped daily through my body. The intensity and frequency of my orgasms quickly reduced; my body became uninterested in itself. Still, I persisted in my quest. Once I had secured the suitable lad to break me open, I eventually confessed to him my secret. He was reluctant, thinking he should know me better before I let him tear me open. But I endured, he took me on one date; then, on our second outing, I let him in me.

I wore black stockings, a scarlet coat with white fur trim and tight, black dress—a uniform I thought suitably pleasing for him. Now I wonder if I looked more like a Christmas ornament than a woman. I asked that we skip the formalities, preferring to return to his bedroom rather than having forced conversation in some tacky bar. He was naturally nervous, even hesitant—but carried on all the same. We shut the door, removed our clothes and he pressed himself up against my open legs.

How unfamiliar it was to finally be torn open! I felt pain, of course, but the pressure of inertia was quickly released, my hole dilated and it gushed out all the toxic fluid I had wrapped myself in for so many years. Gradually, as weeks passed, I began to enjoy the influence of his body and noticed that I began to crave the impact of this man—my sexual drive developing literally within my vagina. Though it never did stray completely from my clitoris. In effect, they became bound together.

My man and I were effortless together; there was little that obligated us—but nothing to keep us apart either. He enjoyed my body and was graciously unperturbed at indulging in the full invention, tongue, hand, foot and all. Rewarded by my perseverance to break myself open, I dumped him after some two months, happy to be torn open and available to whomever I saw fit.

I then refused the presence of contraceptives. Who was I on this pill? Not a woman with a changing body. My orgasms were lost, the curve of my belly increased—I was constantly melancholic. The heaviness of my former sanguinity, warm foaming blood between my vaginal lips, had been aborted and I hated it. I longed for the return of my monthly flow, the excitement of ovulation, the strange flux of menstruation. I wanted the swell of my breasts, the productive moments of plateau when my body refused upheaval and lay dormant in wait for another dead egg to escape its elastic container. I allowed myself the feel of blood bubbling along the length of my labial lips, the heaviness of a full tampon inside me when I masturbated, the charge of a natural orgasm. I stopped taking the pill.

I didn't care whether I became pregnant or not. I took to swallowing the morning-after pill on the occasions it was warranted and infrequently used a condom. But, I cannot lie—I detest condoms as much as the pill. How I hate the feel of rubber along my vagina, the embarrassed wait for a man to find, open and place a condom over his languished penis. I prefer the spontaneity of sex, the freedom of movement, to be and to have without needing to ensure I am carrying the necessary tablets or balloon. The sublime—without need of purchase, without having to enter into a contract—the chance to gulp down and relish whatever our bodies offer each other.

After I was broken open, I continued to seek out physical intimacy—counting the months in-between encounters and defining myself accomplished or failed according to the length of time passed. I lived in a variety of share houses, each with their own quirks—but I was never able to fully settle. Each household began as a happy unit, but would quickly disintegrate. Small issues like bills, cleaning and noise were never managed effectively by any of us, our communal expectations never quite matching with our individual lifestyles or adolescent insensitivity to those around us. But I maintained a handful of casual jobs in inner-city cafes and bars, and persevered with my studies; always living with the expectation that this period of my life was a further transition. I had lived my entire life in anticipation of the future—why would I consider this period any different from what I had always known? Maturity, happiness and stability were a future event.

I still saw my family regularly—visiting them once or twice a week. They demanded I visit them. My younger sisters were still in school and living at home, my brother—too bored to bother finding work—sat at home all day on his own computer, collecting his dole cheque every other week. When I returned, they liked to announce how wonderful it was to have the family 'together' again. This announcement was made every time I visited, as though my absence produced a void in our happy unit. The behaviour of my parents had not changed. They continued to eat the same meals, my mother still got drunk, my father still went missing at strange hours of the night; but their attitude toward me was different. They were very intent on trying to persuade me to return home—offering regular meals, free board, even an allowance. They took no interest in any stories of my outside life that I brought to the table, interrupting me whenever I tried to introduce the subject of my study, relationships, friends, experiences in my new home, etc. In fact, this never changed. Throughout my undergraduate degree, both my mother and father could never remember exactly what it was that I was studying, and would ask me every time I returned home what the title of my degree was. I would respond each time with the same answer, to which they would then ask: "Right. And where does that lead you?"

As time passed, I became more involved in my outside life, returning home much less often, perhaps once every fortnight or month. I found myself motivated to see them only through guilt—never enjoying their company in the mature, less rebellious way that friends now seemed to have with their parents. There was a void between us. All my parents could ask about was what I was studying, where exactly I worked, and whether or not I was healthy. Then they would shift their eyes back to their precious television, preferring to discuss the tabloid reports at hand rather than anything different or new.

I was still gripped with intrusive thoughts of my father abusing me and strange memories would often reveal themselves in my bed—particularly after I had returned home or sat in the car with my father. But I ignored them and tried to squash the thoughts whenever they randomly popped up.

* * *

I still ripped at the skin of my labia. That habit did not subside until I confronted it directly. I was almost always afflicted with inflamed genitalia. I began to have trouble cleaning myself. Like an infant, I was forced to carry wet wipes and zinc oxide cream everywhere I went, applying the paste to reduce the feel of burning flesh. I could never manage to completely rid myself of faecal matter after defecating—I would furiously wipe, sometimes using up to an entire roll of toilet paper, but it seemed a small patch of brown jelly persisted in its phantom apparitions, usually ending up as a thick streak inside my underwear. I became so frightened whenever the possibility of sex materialised that I would quickly retreat to the toilet to clean myself, desperately attempting removal of whatever blood, pus and shit still lingered around my white globe. The repetitive scratching meant that my labia were constantly infected and would leak a vile yellow pus onto my underwear, causing the cloth to fasten itself to my infected skin—an act which only increased the intensity of the wound. The fervent wiping and excessive use of harsh, cheap toilet paper caused my rectum to develop haemorrhoids that bled and, because I refused to have the area examined, any attempts at being completely clean or comfortable were almost impossible.

The sex that ensued after I detached myself from the privacy of the bathroom was always conducted with a certain degree of terror. The men were never obviously suspicious of my actions in the bathroom, but must have secretly questioned my nervous aura. The fear that the man might discover the shame of my genitals meant I could do little more than lie in a state of paralysis when he was fucking me, a dead fish at low tide, until he completed his action and I feigned satisfaction.

My first vice was obsession. When I came upon some person I thought able to fulfil my expectations, I was struck down by this cruel phantom. From the plague of my mind, I gave them a mask: love, adoration, empathy, true care were their unfailing attributes. I tricked myself into believing that fusion with my beloved would quell my psychic storm, that there was such a thing as *meant to be*. Of course, this phantom is a farce; the person, the obsession was nothing more than my abyss, a jagged hole that couldn't possibly be filled by some slimy sexual encounter. I never realised this until it was too late, repeating the same obsessive desire, which was always followed by rejection. It could be triggered within me by a friendly conversation, a small glance, a closed smile, a crinkled nose. It could sometimes take more if I felt strong, then it might take some real display of affection, a private photograph, a handful of dates, a few rounds of sex. But I always became overwhelmed and began to think irrationally, oddly, fantastically—we would be together, our children will be beautiful, we will live together, we will be in love.

I obsessed over the heave of his chest when he raised his body off mine, the sight of his arms tightening, the scowl on his face when he released himself into me. I might have only just met him: he glanced over at me while we were waiting for the bus, his satchel lazily slung across his shoulder, silver wrist watch reminding him that work begins soon, that he has responsibilities. I cock my chin, blink quickly, arch my back. He knows what that means. I want us to turn around, leave the bus stop, fall back into my soft mattress and forget about work. I need to relive that moment, see his back arch again, his wink, his mouth slightly ajar. Then I will feel calm again. I need to be in constant contact, hear their voice, see them, where are you. They are all I think about, in my sleep I dream about them coming to me, embracing me—I feel good, awash with pleasure. I think they are the one for me, they will fulfil me, we can fulfil each other.

I want this stranger to stay forever. He never does.

How irrational, how narcissistic, how fanatical! As if this smashed unconscious would do any good for them. My neuroses, my bizarreness only got worse—I don't want to continue with my infatuation, but I am almost powerless to stop it. I feel out of control. I think, very clearly, "I will get over them. I want them gone". These thoughts did nothing but make it worse. I refreshed my email over and over; I checked my messages as soon as I woke up to see if there was anything. I sent them little tidbits, pieces of information I knew they couldn't resist, that they would always reply to. I asked questions that demanded answers. I gently probed and became neurotic, suspended in a state of hyper-anxiousness until I received a reply. I needed to see them, I needed to be with them again. They must think I am insane. Am I insane?

The witch comes back, my mind makes a racket.

But I had also seen the other side of this whirlpool. The boys that never dare to communicate objectively. Sheepish Australians who prefer to torture their prey by being evasive. Their psychotic circle of adoration always followed by hostility when I don't respond with the answer they desire: recognition of their power. It is impossible to communicate any honest reaction to these dirty fetishists. A caricature is made of my response: my happiness, my jokes, my activities something for them to make their own, to share with me in their private world. I knew what they were doing. I felt it intensely when I fell asleep—their thoughts stretched out to mine across the expanse between us, effortlessly falling inside the open cloth of my pajamas. I wanted it off me. I was unstoppably bonded with the person. I couldn't escape. But I could not ignore the provocative suggestion that perhaps I was just as involved in this as they were.

Then, I acquired a boyfriend.

First, he was nothing but an apparition—an acquaintance I had met through some mutual friends. I knew what was coming. I stopped being able to smell anything without thinking about what type of air his nostrils were sucking in. It took one small look, a brief connection between our wandering eyes, for a chasm to open up beneath me, the juice that had always kept me going—kept my heart beating, my brain ticking—drained into the abyss below. I felt it slip out of me, but I was incompetent to do anything about it. I packed the newborn void with all imaginable recourses to fantasy: cut grass, burnt coffee, freshly painted nails, everything existed for his anticipated proposition. Tight blankets around my body became his arms, his throbbing chest. I enveloped myself in the wish for his warmth. He was there when I stepped onto a train in the lonely morning, when I cycled through an empty park, when I examined vegetables at the market. I hallucinated conversations: of affection, of refusal, of antagonism, of misery. My mind reeled within our pretend discourse—I rambled through moments of potential, rupture, awakening, orgasm. I thought about him when I compelled my body, but I could never quite hold onto the thought. Just as the reality of his glance was exhausted, my thoughts of his wandering hand diminished in a matter of seconds. What if he rejected my desire? Faint but articulate suggestions that this fantasy of coupling might just be 'all in my head' were greeted with major depression. I became useless, a soggy dishrag; my purpose was now disposal. I pondered the effects of gravity on my fragile body, how forces of speeding cars would whip me into pudding. I didn't step off the edge, but the thoughts were intimate. All this because he had done nothing but look at me once.

My hyperbolic arbitration over his teasing look—did he know his power? I fought to stay afloat and my charms, in this instance, were sufficient. Tasty replies, hints, stares, obvious leans morphed into reality. There could be no denial now; his purpose and mine were interlocking. Confiscated life was returned—perhaps he felt the same emptiness too? Either way, I was presented with an offer for nocturnal rendezvous and I quickly forgot my fanaticism. Several drinks later and we lay, now a couple, vacantly possessed by our adjacent bodies.

Psychic violence stumbled into a traumatic affair. It took off rapidly: how was I able to breathe without him before? We never separated—assisted by telegraph lines, satellites, calendars—in our quest for fusion. Solids, liquids, gases were shared: we bathed in each other's piss and dioxide. I stopped shutting the door when I used the toilet. I wanted him to see me, to know that he sucked in my acrid gas. He sublimated his energies with hesitant licks around my anus, fast thrusts of his hips beyond my vaginal cavity—he pretended that he slipped in the juice I provided him, but we all know that is a lie—his need to fuse with the entirety of my body drew him into that rotten hole.

Sloth: all work required additional mental effort. We slept most of the day, engorged our bodies with oily foodstuffs, kept up our intoxication. We skipped out on other events for the sake of more time spent with our bodies pressed tightly together. We stopped drinking, socialising. Interaction seemed unnecessary when we had each other. We both thought that this relationship would surely spark some fantastic development of global proportions. We were powerful, extraordinary, a united force. We compared ourselves to other couples, Sid and Nancy, Jean-Luc and Anna, Patti and Robert, Bonnie and Clyde. We were great thinkers, creators, philosophers, and we raged into the night with long conversations about how to change the world, how to influence our friends' deficiencies.

I tried to give him mouth-to-mouth resuscitation, inflating his lungs with puffs of my air, wondering what it would feel like to have your lungs pop like a balloon.

I ignored the indolent new lumps of fat over my body—he masturbated into the toilet when I showered.

It took time, but he began to revolt me. The smell of his unwashed balls, the thrust of his hips pushing his groin into my face caused a disgust that I keep secret at first. I made him fuck me between my breasts, thinking that perhaps being covered in his white syrup wouldn't feel so bad. I rolled over after sex. Trapped, my whole body stuck in some quicksand from which I could envision escape, but which seemed impossible in the reality of our communion. I used to think his thin and wiry frame quite romantic, charming, wistful. But now his body rocked back and forth in the cradle of my hips and he let out a quick groan after only a few minutes. I wanted him to hurry in his orgasm, I wanted him and his seed out of my body. I jumped up to wash while he lay panting on the bed, his bold, red penis softly throbbing against his white, translucent skin.

He wanted to lick me, but it only produced lack. Invention had vanished. Vaginal penetration became all that was left for both of us to do. He wanted it regularly, then not at all. Our rhythms changed. We lay in bed, masturbating when we thought the other was asleep. We rarely left the house, preferring commercial television to the world. The intense conversations we had quickly evaporated and condensed into real arguments. He ignored the pus in my underwear and that I pulled at my hair for hours on end—only intervening when we were in public and he was embarrassed. I was annoyed by his voice, his gestures, the way he ate. I gorged on fatty meals, stopped bothering to properly cleanse myself after defecation, dressed myself unflatteringly. We couldn't stand each other, but we refused to leave. I asked if he wanted to sleep with other women and tried to set him up accordingly—but he was disgusted by my actions. "Don't you know that I love you?" I thought orgies would be fun, that they might inject me with the excitement I craved.

Apolitical monotony—those endless conversations that followed with friends—"Didn't he love you?", "He's a nice man", "He's a bum, he doesn't have a job", "He hardly calls", "He cheated on you!" These ensued for months, even years, in a psychedelic loop that transcended space and time. Somehow Outer Space is less vacuous; at least it has the vast expanse of the infinite to sustain its dogma. But I felt it; I knew my body could not sustain itself without at least some fantasy of romance. Frightening to be motivated by synthesis in parturiency, separation and union—but I cycle through city parks and gaze upon the lovers entangled on the grass, wanting that for myself, for some man to penetrate me in the open air and announce my return.

I couldn't care that he loved me; I just wanted his body away from me. He stood in front of me on a crowded train. Jammed in by fistfuls of people, he faced me front on—his legs spread apart, arms above his head to steady himself with the handrail. But I knew the secret meaning of his gesture: he lurched over me, he liked me trapped in this place, his body suffocating mine. His face wore a blank look, his mouth was slightly open, his eyes glazed—pure primal reaction to my withdrawal. I shifted to the side, trying to escape his bodily idiom, but it was no use. There was nowhere that I could turn without being encompassed by him.

I left him with sudden violence. He didn't leave his house for almost a month. I returned to the wild company of friends. I revisited the sacred calendar, and The Theory of Weekend became my orthodoxy. I drank until I could no longer stand, subscribing to the ritual that vomit and severe physical disturbance must rule the day after any social event. My nose became a vacuum for white powder—the third dimension through which I could incinerate perception. I no longer wanted to exist as my ordinary self, sucking in enough nitrous oxide until my mouth would foam, my body would collapse and friends would reach for the phone to dial an ambulance. I had visions where I would rise up outside of my body, my skin coated with warm prickles and my vagina engorged with blood, arms and legs heavy, filled with oozing hot, wet sand and delicious whipped cream chargers. "If this is what it is like to die, it must not be so bad."

The future and the past seemed blank, empty—I filled both with distant narratives of success, contentment, vague objects at the vanishing point. I came from a family, I was educated—I would never stay in this place of Thursday-Friday-Saturday, this convention would quite naturally stop. The people I lived with were but an ornament to my culture, there was nothing tangible about our interactions. The social world in which I existed—but was at once completely estranged from—was rife with antagonisms and fallings-out, always over minor indiscretions (usually as a result of cheating or borrowed money). Fulfilment, sublimity and exhaustion existed only when I was intoxicated, high or fucking. Repetitive banality was lived as though our actions were extraordinary: *de rigueur* to frequent the same bars, mingle with the same people, witness young bodies force themselves into a chemical stupor. These were the celebrated actions of teenage wildlife.

I could not picture my body and was continuously surprised by the sight of it in the mirror. I experienced a sudden sense of unfamiliarity, particularly when I saw my face in photographs. I would take photos of my face from many angles, pouting, smiling, attempting the blank but extroverted poses of fashion models. My online profile became a tomb for images of my face: time recorded my conscious wish to electronically preserve my structure. But I was rarely happy with the photos it produced and took to capturing hundreds of pictures, in the vain attempt to secure a representation of myself that was an intact vision of my desire.

I missed the constant company of my former lover and wished I had someone to live with from whom I didn't feel estranged. Banal, but I will confess to you how I had fantasies of marriage, a career, a large house. Everyone wants their future secured by an eternal present.

I returned to my schedule, keeping check of how many times I had sex in the year. It had been a good year, perhaps a dozen or more men and women had slept with me. I then began sleeping with a local boy to whom I was not terribly attracted, but I liked knowing that I had access to regular sex. Also, I enjoyed the familiarity of our routine. We would meet at his house every other night: eat, drink, talk and pass out. Around 5am, he would roll over and slip a lone finger around the elastic of my underwear and start to gently rub my clitoris until I woke from sleeping. Then he would pull off my underwear, roll me on my back and fuck me until he was satisfied. Then he would roll back over and fall asleep. I would feign pleasure in all this, but was equally unable to ignore the fact that my desire evaporated as soon as he entered me. I had trouble identifying when he was finished; he had more control over his body than I was used to in a man and would not come so quickly. I limited the force with which I rocked back and forth on top of him, because I thought that after fifteen minutes he would surely be done and I could get off him. He opened his eyes and gave me a cutting look. "Well, I guess he wasn't finished!" I made him fuck me on top instead.

I would scratch at my vulva when he was asleep. It became so inflamed and constantly weeping pus and sticky blood that it caused the lining of my underwear to be permanently stained a dark yellow. He did not notice how I would rip back large chunks of thick skin from my groin, rolling it up in a yellow ball and staring until I decided to quietly dispossess myself of it. I would watch him when he was sleeping, feeling that I should recognise our estrangement, his obvious lack of interest. But, particularly after he fucked me, I would be overcome with a wave of emotion. My brain hiccupped involuntary musings on engagement, marriage, coupling, babies. I was confused by this, but indulged it all the same.

We never used protection. When I missed my period for two months, began having cramps and experiencing nausea, I became nervous. I felt trapped in the confines of this strange relationship—keeping my legs and heart open for a man for whom I felt very little. Yet I wanted him to stay with me and retain the familiar, to continue the routine and feel connected. I awaited the results of my blood test and secretly hoped that I might be pregnant, quietly talking to my stomach, feeling as though my body would soon split in two.

The test came back negative and he dumped me.

I had broken my body. My labia were eternally red, raw, bleeding from the effects of my nails clawing at it; my hair was falling out, thin and worn because I had become so immersed in its infinite inconsistencies. My eyes were strained; my neck and back always sore. I had no interest in the presentation of my body, in my behaviour, in what I was becoming. I lived in a state of intoxication—numbed, but elated, by the falsity of my world. I was alone, with an untenable desire to become a mother and a predictable need for sanctuary at the expense of my own body. The voice inside me was, for once, clear. I took action, deciding that the start of my adult life should not be defined by destruction or paradox. I sought therapy.

* * *

My first experience in therapy as a child, despite the bizarre predictions made by the counsellor, had opened up the possibility of my own voice. I had always felt a natural pull back to that place where I could express one thousand tiny fragments without any need for adhesive, where the person opposite did nothing but soak in my words. I had felt this, too, in my intense conversations with my English teacher, and wanted to return to that place—only this time I wanted to be more honest. I had read some psychology and knew my repetitive behaviour was the effect of some emotional imbalance. I saw the stories I offered myself: to continue living in the world of shallow intoxication—parties, social events, inert conversation, tedious employment—or, to push forward and experiment with possibility. I chose the latter. I saw my physician and was referred to a female psychiatrist.

The shrink was named Adelaide—an odd name for an odd woman. She was bright, with the aura of a witch or sorcerer, and seemed to delight in adorning her body in large pieces of scarlet resin. She had a fierce exterior and usually would do little more than stare at me while I talked at her for an hour. I saw her once a week for two years.

I would think she knew what I was going to say, but was almost always wrong. At times it seemed clear that she was not listening, but that was besides the point. It wasn't up to her to carry me through, I didn't need a mother—I needed somebody to help reconstruct my psyche.

Hours and hours of therapy passed and I began to hear the sound of my voice, my clichéd stories, how I had woven the hum of my existence into a neat package. The power of an exchange between a woman doing nothing but listening and a patient offering up their thoughts quickly disassembled my unconscious constructions. Realising the stupidity of myself, the destructiveness through which I operated, the irrationality of my behaviour, caused me, at first, to seriously consider, and then attempt, suicide. Adelaide had given me her number, non-addictive tranquilisers and the reassurance of a better future; the sanctity of her distance provided me with what I needed. I persevered, powered initially by my need for a relationship and, then, by the force of my own voice. I persisted in my battle with myself.

Oh, sorry, I have lied to you again! I like to tell grand stories of redemption, salvation, how the Lord Jesus Christ must have blessed my soul. I was, of course, completely obsessed with Adelaide. I had deep fantasies that she could be my mother, my sister—I tried to think about what it might be like to fuck her, but this thought didn't seem to fit in the logic of our relationship. Sometimes she would spark up, particularly when I told her about my interactions with women, but the charge in our transference was too entangled for me to clearly distinguish anything for you. I managed to find out where she lived, what her mother looked like, who her father was—a fact that I confessed to her. Her response: "Well, what are you going to do? Show up at my door?"

Therapy was a miserable nightmare. The previously ignored voice that had screamed unanswerable memories of my father's erection, of him fondling me under the fence, suffocating me with his lips, came back with the force of a thermonuclear implosion.

I was lying in bed. I do not remember what I was thinking about, or how I might have managed to accept that perhaps the strange, intrusive visions I regularly had might have been real. My father would sometimes drive me back to my house, and when we sat in the car I would think, almost in a panic, "Run! You have to get away from him". He had done nothing to me, I thought: "Why would my mind suddenly race?" Then, the flood of memories materialised and, this time, I did not try to push them away or ignore them. Why would I panic when I was around my father, why would I be so afraid that he was watching me every time I bathed, why had I gripped onto the blankets so tightly my whole life? I remembered his mouth, his voice, his red penis, his gripped hand, his aggression, and I absorbed the fragments of vision my mind reeled over-and-over for me. At this moment, I paid attention to myself.

Shortly after this event, I began to attack my body with greater ferocity than ever before. I would take a butcher knife to hack into the flesh of my arm—watching the chunks of skin peel back from red flesh. I let a boy masturbate and come all over my body after we got drunk together. I lay silently next to him, not daring to even attempt to respond to his gesture throughout our exchange. He finished quickly and left, almost immediately. The sharpness of his physical exorcism, his ignorance of me, my impotence, the fact that I was drunk and covered in semen, now alone, prompted me to seek out the sharpest knife in the kitchen and retreat to my empty room. I took the blade, at first slowly dragging it along the length of my forearm. I stared as a thin streak of red blood rose to the surface of my skin, the white lace of newly dead flesh hung over the edge. I pulled the knife above my head and lowered it quickly, watching the blade hack into my skin. I could not cut very deep—I was a faker, impotent even in my attempt to open up my own body. But I marked myself with blood, a lattice of cuts and flecks of dead skin. I fell asleep, wishing that I could be more able to commit penetrable violence against my body.

I was offered psychiatric drugs. I accepted without much consideration. A strange concoction, the anti-depressant. I had taken many drugs before, but was curious to try these ones. I was not always comfortable with my narcissistic destruction, and felt that facing the fact of my father's abuse would require some form of aid. The side-effects of my prescribed drugs were heinous, causing me to switch medications many times. At first, I gained weight—perhaps around twenty kilograms. It happened slowly: an increased appetite, continued lack of physical exertion, constipation bought on by the medication, plus the tablets themselves affected the gross expansion of my body. I wondered out aloud, to Adelaide, what Freud might say about a psychiatric drug that caused the patient to hold on to her toxins. She just smiled warmly: "What are you going to do, then?" The tablets also gave me terrible nervous shocks. I was regularly disturbed from feelings of electrocution, as though a laser was pulsating through my nervous system and destroying it from the inside. But I persisted in swallowing the drug and was graciously relieved of my anxiety. The intrusive thoughts, in particular, evaporated—I was no longer was crippled by interruptions of imminent death, kidnap, destruction. Some relief from my anguish was welcome.

My drinking continued, perhaps even worse than before. I submitted to my depression—forcing alcohol down my throat in a quest for bodily expulsion. Parties, clubs, gigs became my refuge—a place where conversation was throttled by the thunder of music, friendship soured by the presence of vomit, the unconscious drives constantly on display. I had accepted that I needed to distance myself from my family if I was to persevere toward any kind of happiness and create an image of myself. But, what is a person without a family? I walked away from a midnight party, my friends—in the drunken haze—not noticing my sudden disappearance. I had ingested a copious amount of spirits and smoked continuously from a hash pipe the entire evening. I stepped out into the middle of a busy highway, watching a blur of screeching cars swerve around my fraught body. I was sent into a panic, did I really want to whip my body through a blender? My mind answered then, very clearly: "Yes."

I was pulled back off the road by a person I did not know and led to an emergency room. The movement of traffic returned to normal, drivers continued on their way without the fear that they might be used in some girl's crazy experiment to see what happens when a tonne of metal hits a flaccid organism. I sat down at the counter and told the nurse that I wanted to kill myself, and that if I were left alone I would probably do it. "What drugs have you taken?" was her response. I couldn't convince her of my logic. I was admitted, given fluids, dressed in a robe and told to wait for a psychiatrist.

In the process of waiting I found a bulldog clip—the kind with a metal edge. I bitterly dragged the clip across my wrist and tried to pulverise my flesh. Like a naughty child, I peeped out from behind the partition. The doctor caught sight of me and saw what I was doing. She rubbed my head: "Poor child, the counsellor will come to you soon." She took the clip with her and left the curtain open so that I was exposed to everyone who walked passed—but I could also see out into the hospital. I had to wait for hours until a doctor finally arrived, so I had time to watch the department perform for me. I did not sleep, but shifted between fits of crying and silence—occasionally taking the opportunity to just lie and stare at my hands.

Perhaps it was due to the fact that it was 3am in an overcrowded public emergency room. The psychiatrist came, took one look at me, and said: "What has happened to you has happened to a lot of people, you are nothing special." Then he left. He left me there for a long time, howling like a wounded animal from his response. Several hours later another psychiatrist, this one with a disturbing body odour, attended to me.

"What happened to you?" I tried to explain, as best I could to this foul man, that my life was in fact worth nothing, that I was completely logical in my wish for death. "My father used to touch me, my mother didn't care." He wanted to know what exactly had triggered the episode. He knew about the hash I had smoked that night, about my intoxication, but there was something else that I wasn't confessing to him. I relented:

"It's my birthday."

Well, if the force of my immaturity did not strike me then like a bolt of lighting, I might never have been spared. Birthdays had always been my happy occasion, a saturation of presents and attention; but on this year I was estranged from everyone, because I was so depressed, and received almost nothing. Confronted with my autonomy on the night meant for social collectivity had led me into this institution. I had returned to the place from whence I came, my communal foundation and, amongst the sounds of the truly ill, the dying and the committed hypochondriacs, I made a choice. I called the psychiatrist. He wanted to admit me to his facility, but I refused his offer of admission. I left the hospital— walking through the cold Sunday morning the rest of the way home.

Before I left, he said to me: "The dealer has handed you a wrinkled pair of cards. You can smooth them out as best you can, but they will always be wrinkled."

"Well, fuck you."

* * *

What happened next? I suppose it is obvious to you that I have never been in love: how could that be possible given the condition of my body? I think about it all the time, of course, some man riding in on a white horse with the keys to his château. Actually, better if it was a manual car. A horse would be stupid and I find nothing more attractive than watching a man take control of his machine. But let's forget this whimsical fantasy and move on to something idiosyncratic.

I could no longer study without taking regular breaks to masturbate. I got bored easily: the onslaught of reading material and formulaic exercises sent me into a sleepy haze. I stopped sleeping with so many people, but the intensity of my sexual energy persisted. I met a few people through online networks for sex, but felt unaffected by their libido. I had no wish to return to the place of forced copulation. I began sharing live videos of myself to my online friend, Alain. I liked to perform my body for him, watching myself through the screen. Of course, I wanted to push up myself against him on the other side ... but it was all the more enticing to me that his body was too far apart for us to fulfil each other. We opened our legs instead and did it to ourselves, filming as we went, knowing the other was watching this private home-made spectacle. The invisible electronic wall allowed us to be as graphic as we liked, as demanding as necessary, and I moved beyond boundaries I might otherwise not have traversed. If I asked him to push his hand inside his dark tunnel and describe it, then he would. He wanted to see me bend over, perched on the edge of my bed, glancing back at the camera, exposed like a peacock.

I reasoned: why should I have felt ashamed? Why keep my sexuality contained and expressed in the sanctity of a darkened bedroom with some foolish boy who knows only how to force a moment's pleasure by pushing semen out of himself? Alain was someone who, on the surface of things, was sleazy. He was not a person who took and did not return. He worshipped the female body in its entirety, its every hair, hole, pore and sanctum, his whole body moved by the force of his desire. He made videos for me, mostly of him masturbating. He lay back on his bed, panting through his thick accent, rocking his hand back and forth across his cock, lowering his fingers and rubbing his balls, taking pleasure in the feel of his chest, nipples, hips. He would call my name, sometimes glancing at the camera. He zoomed into the head of his dick, now spewing ejaculate all over his stomach and chest. When he moaned, a little shiver ran over his body.

It was here that I confronted the relationship I had with my asshole. Why should this place be so secretive, so mysterious and horrific? Why exist as an extraterrestrial in my own body, unable to even possess myself? Alain told me it should be another place where I could find pleasure, serious pleasure, in my body—and I took heed. The tightness, its warmth, the peculiar sensations it gave me—it could be as sensitive as the underside of my foot—but it seemed connected by twisting nerves to my whole body, like I felt everything contract and expand in rapture whenever a tongue or a penis passed over the vulnerable flesh. It also enabled me to enact a more active role. I could penetrate my partner, watch him squirm with delight when I thrust a finger deep into his little wrinkled anus.

I suppose the presence of shit in my sexual life was a problem in the beginning, but—like the thick, brown hair that grazed the inside of my genitals, the strange, rubbery feel of pre-cum, or the taste of my partner kissing me just after he has eaten me out—I got over it. I began to finger myself when I masturbated, letting myself rub my asshole— at first with the same trepidation as when I discovered my vagina years earlier - but I pursued it all in the name of pleasure. I had some inkling of the potentials for that hole, those times when tongues and fingers had strayed too far from their intended destination, swiping a quick but magnificent stroke over the rectum. But these were nothing in comparison to the unrestrained burst I felt when I let a man penetrate my asshole, let him lick at it; or when I bent over before a camera, pulled at the sides of my cheeks and fashioned myself open and exposed.

* * *

A superlative energy seemed to exist all around me, the unspoken. I could not help but immerse myself in the charged nature of the everyday, the strange sexual agenda of conversation, friendship, plane-travel, education. What was I to do with this energy? In truth, I began to indulge it to the fullest degree.

Lecture theatres, in particular, seem continuously charged with tacit energy. In a decrepit 1970s lecture hall, I found the eyes of the speaker repeatedly returning his gaze to mine. I could not make sense of his voice; the message he was trying to pass to the small group of listeners was difficult in its syntax and required full attention. But his ocean-blue eyes were more interesting to me, anyway. Did he know I couldn't listen because of him? I looked around at the other students and saw how they eagerly took notes, but a few scattered throughout the audience also seemed seduced and abandoned, as though we all would rather stand up in unison and carry our speaker out, over our heads, to the back of the hall in a ceremony to return to dominance. I can't even pretend to mimic the listeners' behaviour—I will sit here and fantasise instead. I groped his lean arms, the force of his voice, the laptop computer he kept fiddling with—what secrets does his computer hold? I argue with the frivolity of my actions: I should be listening, I should be trying to understand what he is saying, but we keep staring at each other and he knows how caustic this eye-dance has become—there is no way I will be able to comprehend today's lesson.

Comprehension has never been my strength. How can I manage to see all the possible outcomes when it seems that so many can exist? I made love, quite impulsively, to a close female friend once. I knew it was coming, but of course I didn't. How could I, when we had spent the entire duration of our friendship bathed in a cocktail of deep conversation, frivolous humour, unspoken lust and forced separation? She was beautiful, and she knew it. She wore her body like a cat, hanging her tail in the air, proud to put the force of her presence on display to her admirers. I loved her—who wouldn't?—but it was the kind of love one can slide into without any wellspring or convention. It was a close friendship and we respected it as such.

So our quiet passion unfolded spontaneously. Of course, alcohol was involved—an unfortunate prerequisite to overcoming unspoken hurdles—but it was not the catalyst. Months, even years, of indirect stares, sublimated conversation and pale affections crystallised one night in her bed. It was shallow at first. We lay pressed up against each other. She pushed her backside deep into my hips and tightened my arm around her waist—this could be forgotten as a signal of close friendship, drunk together on a cold Saturday night—but our lungs quickened. I could feel her heavy pulse through her thin cloth. Her hand lowered and glazed over the skin of my thigh—there could be no mistaking this gesture. Shifting my legs open, she followed the signal and penetrated me, deep into the black moistness, turning her face into mine so that our lips met. Our encounter was brief, with the usual giggling anxiety that follows sudden sublimity—but the energy continued. We remain devoted to each other.

* * *

I could tell you everything about my body. I could tell you how it tried to align itself with the American quest for self-esteem through a public autopsy—I suppose I just did that when I told you about my asshole—but the complexity of its function will not be neutered by the presence of pleasure. Remember I said that I had never been in love? It's probably true. The history of my body has made me a recluse. I cannot abandon my body. To see my faults, the cracks between the paragraphs of this history, is not to suffer needlessly, but to turn a page in opposition.

www.ingramcontent.com/pod-product-compliance
Lightning Source LLC
Chambersburg PA
CBHW020025030726
47499CB00007B/2272